RDEN'S
TOUCH

An Evans Novel of Romance

ARDEN'S TOUCH

BETH HENDERSON

M. EVANS & COMPANY NEW YORK

Library of Congress Cataloging-in-Publication Data

Henderson, Beth.

Arden's touch / Beth Henderson.
p.   cm. — (An Evans novel of romance)
ISBN 0-87131-640-4 : $15.95
I. Title.   II. Series.
PS3558.E4823A87   1990
813'.54—dc20   90-20177
CIP

M. Evans and Company, Inc.
216 East 49 Street
New York, New York 10017

Manufactured in the United States of America

9 8 7 6 5 4 3 2 1

Dedicated to Christiane Heggan
who is always there to boost my spirits
and offer much-needed advice.
Thanks, Chris!

Prologue
Scotland, 1603.

THE HALLWAY ECHOED with the *tromp* of booted feet and the rattle of swords in scabbards. A company of shadows marched with the men, leaping and shifting with the erratic, wavering flames of the torches the soldiers carried. Each man was heavily armed, ready for battle. Yet only one man's eyes glittered with eagerness and hatred.

He strode ahead of the men. His long legs covered the distance to the bedchamber quickly. The rich, dark clothing he wore made him a brother to the night. Or perhaps, as his men thought, a sibling of the devil. His appearance enhanced this superstition for his raven beard was trimmed to an aristocratic point, and his austere features were sharpened by the stark, starched ruff that framed his swarthy face.

He stopped abruptly, startling the guards at his heels, and gestured to a thick oak door. "Open it!" His lip curled in derision. His dark eyes burned in the firelight, a mirror image of hell.

The men were uneasy. Highland-bred, they feared nothing. Nothing, that is, but this cold man from the south: an Englishman. Reluctantly, a guard pushed at the door. The stout planks refused to budge. He stepped back, relieved. "'Tis locked," he said.

The Englishman's scowl darkened. "Break it down."

The kilted warriors exchanged furtive glances. "The mistress . . ." one protested.

"Break it down!"

Still the men hesitated, knowing what they would find on this midnight crusade, knowing death hovered near on impatient wings.

The man swore at his underlings. All of them were men of the MacCrimmon clan. They had never relished bowing to his commands, nor had the witch he had wed at the queen's command. God's teeth! If he had known taking Mary MacCrimmon's hand would have led to this day, he would have thwarted Elizabeth Tudor's desires and refused the gift of this highland estate. With James now on the throne he would probably lose what little he had gained. James Stuart had already shown that Mary MacCrimmon's nephew was one of his favorites.

Goaded by the stoic loyalty of the clansmen, the Englishman drew his own sword and kicked the door in.

Inside the room his wife sat among passion-twisted sheets, her thick, auburn hair swirling enticingly about her naked shoulders. The quick rise and fall of the bed sheet she clutched to her breast was the only sign of agitation, for her expression was calm. Proud even in dishabille, Mary MacCrimmon awaited her fate.

Next to the bed stood her lover, his hastily donned kilt his only covering. A long sword was at the ready in his hand. Defiant, the doomed man grinned at the cuckolded husband.

The identity of his wife's lover infuriated the Englishman. "The piper!" he hissed in disbelief.

Mary MacCrimmon's soft laugh was derisive. "Aye, my lord husband," she purred. "My piper. A far better mon than ye."

His face now red with fury, the Englishman threw his scabbard across the room. His naked blade gleamed in the torch light. "Then go with him to hell, woman," the Englishman growled.

The piper's weapon came up to meet the Englishman's sword. The ringing sound filled the room. It was a death knell for the Scotsman. Although the piper was trained in war, it was soon apparent that the Englishman was by far the superior swordsman. He toyed with his adversary as the clansmen watched silently, unwilling to thwart their master, yet unwilling to take up arms against one of their own.

With a quick flex of his wrist the Englishman disarmed the piper. His sword swung back quickly, sinking deep into the man's heart.

Mary MacCrimmon watched as her lover slumped to the floor. Although her head was still held high, tears ran unheeded down her cheeks. But she did not sob, did not plead with her vengeful husband. Long before her brother had fallen in battle, long before the English queen had interfered with their clan by thrusting an unwanted bridegroom upon the proud MacCrimmon lass, she had promised herself to the piper. Now they would be together in hell.

Her husband turned from his fallen prey, his sword still dripping her lover's blood, and Mary MacCrimmon lifted her chin proudly to meet death.

Chapter One
Kentucky, 1990.

IT WAS A lover's caress; cold, honed steel against warm, living flesh. Tenderly, the blade followed the vulnerable, arched length of the woman's throat, touching but not destroying. . . .

Charlie Arden shivered and grabbed the remote control from her partner's hand. "Nope, that won't do," she declared and hit the power button, sending the screen to black. "I don't think our audience is up for anything that blood-chilling."

Jack Donahue shrugged and moved across the office to rewind the tape in the VCR. "If we don't do horror movies, what will we do for the Halloween show?"

"God only knows." Charlie leaned forward in her chair, elbows on knees, hands in her red curls.

"Witches' sabbaths? Devil cults?" Jack hunkered down before the TV, watching the counter tick off the numbers, backwards. "Seances, black magic, vampires, werewolves, curse of the mummy . . ."

Charlie looked up. "Have we ever done Egyptian curses?"

Jack grinned back over his shoulder. "Do we *want* to do them?"

Frustrated, she ran her hands through her hair. Her short curls bounced back into place. "No, we don't. What have they got to do with Halloween? Or Kentucky, for that matter? We need the local tie-in."

The movie finished rewinding. "We've got three weeks," he reminded.

Charlie rose to her feet, stretching. "Our reputation's on the line, Jack. We'll never make it." Ever since *On Assignment* had aired three years ago, the team of Arden and Donahue had kept Louisville audiences tuning into Channel 5 every Sunday. The stories they presented were humorous, thought-provoking, and sometimes tragic. But the segments had all been geared to the southwestern Kentucky audience, with a format that was entertaining as well as informative.

Jack watched his partner's reflection in the TV screen. Tall, slim, and beautiful—that was Charlie Arden. A three-time winner of the Kentucky Broadcaster of the Year award, Charlie also had the most lusted after legs in the business, though it was an attribute that was hidden behind the news desk every night. Louisville audiences only saw her enchanting dimple as she smiled, wishing them a good night.

"There's one story we haven't done," Donahue said. "Ghosts."

"Ghosts? Might as well do haunted houses," she declared in disgust.

"Word travels fast," a deep voice said from the doorway. Stan Powers, the news director, loosened his tie and stepped into the office. "How did you find out? I just heard about it myself." With a secretive air, Stan pushed the door closed behind him. His wispy brown hair fanned out above his ears from a growing bald spot, adding to his usual harried look.

"Heard about what?" Charlie asked.

Stan grinned diabolically. "The haunted house."

She groaned.

Stan laughed and made himself at home behind her desk.

"Somehow I knew that would be your response."

"It's too . . . too . . ." She searched for a word.

Stan picked up a pencil and dropped it point down against the papers on the desk top. His eyes were on the #2 rather than on the two reporters. "NAB calls it apropos."

"North American Broadcasting, huh?" Jack mused. He pulled up a second chair and settled in, propping his size fourteen loafers on one corner of the desk.

"The network is sending a crew here to cover a haunted house?" Charlie asked.

"Not exactly." Stan studied the pencil a moment or two more. "They want you to do a story on it, Charlie."

Her blue eyes widened. "The network?"

Jack whistled softly. "The big time. I knew they'd call you one day, Chuck." Only Jack ever called her Chuck. They'd been working together for five years now. She had danced at his wedding and had kept busy ever since then turning down the blind dates his wife arranged for her. Ginny Donahue still couldn't believe that there was a woman alive who could resist her blond husband's boyish grin and gangly physique. It was inconceivable to her that the affection between the partners was entirely platonic. Not that Jack had always wanted it that way. It was Charlie who drew the line in their partnership.

Charlie shook her head adamantly. "No, we work as a team. Both of us or nothing."

"Ignore her," Jack said to his boss. "We both know I'm just a cameraman. She's the brains."

"So work together on it," Stan said.

"On a haunted house?" Charlie insisted. "Give me a break, Stan."

The news director leaned back in his chair. "That's exactly what I am doing, Charlie. The network wants you to do this story for Halloween. If it meets their requirements, you go to Chicago."

Charlie looked over at her partner.

"No," Jack said. "Those aren't my awards hanging on that wall. You are going. Not me. I stay here."

"It depends on the story, doesn't it?" She turned back to Stan. "Why would I want to leave Channel 5, anyway? Louisville is the forty-second market."

"And a nationwide news show based in Chicago is chopped liver," Stan said sarcastically. "Don't you even want to know about the haunted house?"

"No. Oh, all right."

"She's prejudiced," Jack warned. "I've suggested ghosts for the Halloween topic for years and she's turned me down flat each time."

Charlie glared at him. "Do we get to use it on our own show?" she asked Stan.

"NAB already cleared it."

She sighed. "And you won't let me do any other story."

"You know me so well." Stan smiled. "I think the location will interest you."

Charlie picked up a notebook from the desk and whisked the pencil from Stan's hand before it could drop again. "It better," she muttered.

Deprived of his prop, the older man laced his fingers across his chest and tilted the chair back until the casters groaned. "I'm sure you've heard of the MacCrimmons," he began.

"Racing magnates," Charlie said. "There's a rumor that one of them is about to throw his hat in the political arena. Now *that* would be a story."

Stan Powers shook his head. He could see it all now: she'd take the assignment, and in the process he'd lose one hell of a reporter. It was still hard to associate this beautiful, efficient, and talented woman with the naive teenager who had once been the soft, seductive voice manning the station switchboard. How eager she had been then. Her brilliant red hair had hung to her waist. Her blue eyes had been wide and innocent beneath long, dark lashes.

At thirty-two Charlie had matured, hardened. The warm, outgoing child had disappeared. Only the professional remained. Her divorce from Philip Wilson five years before had changed Charlie. She had become a social hermit, repulsing all flirtations and advances, living for her job and through it.

"We aren't doing a political update. We are catching ghosts," Stan clarified.

Charlie looked disgusted.

Jack swung his feet down from the desk and leaned forward. "On camera?"

"I would hope so," Stan said.

"Hot damn!" Jack turned to the young woman at his side. "Chuck, we gotta do it. You know what a chance this is? If we can get a genuine spirit photo . . ."

"Genuine?" Charlie closed her eyes and took a deep, exasperated breath. How could they get pictures of a myth? Intelligent people did not believe in the existence of ghosts. It made her wonder about the network executives. Still, there probably was a story in it somewhere. She sighed. "Okay. Where is the haunted house, Stan?"

There was nothing graceful or beautiful about MacCrimmon Manor. Charlie had expected the usual Southern mansion, complete with Doric columns, covered verandas, and gracefully curving staircases. Instead she found a disdainful mausoleum. The dark gray stone building sat on the soil of the Bluegrass State with resentment etched on its centuries-old face. Rising to four stories, the manor boasted steeply sloping slate roofs. Tall, narrow windows stared haughtily at the visitors. Sturdy English ivy reclaimed the outer face of the house, reaching toward the multitude of chimneys that bristled with indignation against a lowland blue sky.

The only feature of MacCrimmon Manor that seemed at home in Kentucky was a pair of horse-head knockers mounted on each of the massive oak doors within the entrance porch.

A tiny wren of a woman answered Jack's knock. She was dressed in brown. Her hair was a gray that matched the stone of the portico. Her tiny black eyes darted excitedly from Jack, to the bright yellow Channel 5 van, to the girl climbing out of the red sports car.

"It's really you," she breathed, rolling the *R* so that it purred. "Charlie Arden from the television."

Charlie stifled an amused smile before striding forward to greet the woman. "I'm afraid so. I believe Gwen Hale is expecting us?"

"Aye, she is that," the wren agreed, her Scots accent thickening. "Come in, come in. I'm Mrs. MacLynn, the housekeeper. Miss Gwen is out, but she and the laird will be back this evening. I'll just get you settled in your rooms."

They followed Mrs. MacLynn into the manor. It was more a museum than a home. Stag heads were mounted high on the dark paneled walls. Crossed swords, battle-axes, and other ancient implements of war shared space with aged portraits of stern men and women dressed in clan tartans. Overhead a chandelier of burnished metal supported a dozen thick candles, their burnt wicks and drippings reflecting use rather than decoration.

Jack nudged Charlie. "They forgot the suits of armor."

"It is quite impressive," she agreed, keeping the pace with the housekeeper. "I understand Ms. Hale is a cousin of the MacCrimmons."

"Third cousin," Mrs. MacLynn explained. "Her grandmother was a MacCrimmon."

"And the laird?"

The housekeeper laughed. "A pet name, Miss Arden.

We've maintained the title as an affectionate designation for the head of the family."

Charlie mounted the staircase a step behind her informant. "That would be Mark MacCrimmon? Is he planning on running for a political office, Mrs. MacLynn?"

"No, miss. That would be Mr. Donald."

"And is he in residence?"

The housekeeper grinned and paused at the top of the stairs. "Ah, but yer a persistent lass," she said. "None lives in the manor but the laird as a rule. But with yer comin' the clan is gatherin'. Both Miss Gwen and Mr. Donald have moved in, and they've brought a guest with them."

"Sounds like a house party," Jack said. "Are we all hunting for ghosts, Mrs. MacLynn?"

The little woman's grin widened. "Now it's not huntin' so much as avoidin', Mr. Donahue. The manor is a very old home and we carried the ghosties with us when Mrs. James MacCrimmon moved the building here. She was a rich American and the present laird's grandmother. But I'm sure Miss Gwen will tell you the family history. This is your room, Miss Arden,"she designated, stopping before a thick oak door. "Mr. Donahue is just across the hall."

The man on horseback watched the cloud of dust approach down the lane. Whoever was driving at least had the decency to go slowly. Which meant it wasn't Gwen at the wheel. He was unfamiliar with the red sports car and only vaguely curious when it pulled to a stop. A woman climbed out and gazed across the fields, her head cocked to one side as if listening. He admired her slim form, the way her jeans fit snugly over nicely rounded hips. Another tourist who'd managed to get past the gates, he mused. He thought they'd cured the estate of trespassers.

As he watched, the intruder climbed on the white fencing and swung her leg over the top rail. "Damn," he muttered.

Was there no end to the gall of these sightseers?

"Determined, isn't she, Madoc?" he asked his gray gelding.

The horse's ears perked at the sound of his master's voice.

The woman dropped into the field and began trotting, her lope easy and unhurried. It wasn't her action so much as her destination that held the watching man's attention. She was making a beeline to the paddock!

"Hell. She needs to be taught a lesson."

As if in agreement, the gray's head nodded. He pranced, sensing the man's irritation.

"Damn right," the man said. "We'll put a little scare into her."

The gray tugged at the bit, anxious to be off. The woman had reached the top of the hill and was disappearing into the wooded area that surrounded the paddock. The man had kept the young stallion secluded there while training progressed. Outside eyes were not welcome. Now it looked as if his effort was about to be a waste of time. With a swift touch of his heel, he sent his horse toward the wood at a gallop.

The drive was long and winding, shaded by the half-skeletoned laurel trees that flanked it on either side. Glimpses of rolling, fenced meadows and grazing horses could be seen between the barked columns. Although her room was comfortably modern in its furnishings, the crisp autumn day had called to Charlie, urging her to explore the estate before tackling the ghost hunt.

Ghosts, for heaven's sake! How could she get her teeth into such an asinine assignment? If this story was supposed to get her a network promotion, she was doomed.

A drive would clear her head, she thought. It was impossible to concentrate on the Halloween show with Stan's carrot of a NAB appointment dangling before her eyes. She wasn't even sure she wanted to leave Channel 5. Or Louisville.

The trumpeting of a stallion drew Charlie from the contemplation of her future. She wasn't ready to face the questions yet, much less find answers. It was far easier to retreat.

The sound of the stallion's challenge transported her to younger days when decisions had been trivial and her abiding interest had been horses. Those happy years before her parents' divorce, before she had met and married Phil Wilson. Her days of innocence.

She let the animal's clarion take her back to her childhood, recalling the treasured afternoons with her father.

Bluegrass born and reared, Charlie had, to her father's delight, been fascinated with horses from the time she could walk. She never missed a chance to accompany him to the stables. Hal Arden was a track official who took pride in knowing the history behind every entry that came to the post at Churchill Downs. His daughter eagerly absorbed it all and, unlike many girls, never outgrew her fascination with horses.

Because of her background, Charlie could easily put together a documentary on racing and thoroughbreds. She mused on the possibility, pulling her cherry-red Impulse to a stop along the lane.

"No Trespassing" signs were nailed with military precision down the expanse of tall, white rail fencing. They marched along the country lane, warning her of prosecution. Beyond them lay a field populated with a few sparse brown stalks, survivors of the harvest.

The shrill call came again. This time she identified its direction: the golden-hued grove at the top of the field.

The breeze stirred the distant trees and tossed her bright curls about her pert, oval face. A few tendrils clung to the dark collar of the flannel shirt she wore beneath her fisherman's sweater.

Charlie ignored the signs. She was on MacCrimmon land on assignment. Surely that negated all posted warnings. A moment later she was scrambling up and over the five-foot fence with ease.

The wild bugle sounded again, piercing the clean, fresh air. Charlie brushed her hand hastily on her jeans, her head cocked toward the sound. The field lacked a track of any sort so she set out across it, crushing the brittle stalks in her path.

The stallion was hidden from the road, but she felt his presence as well as heard his eager call. Another fence blocked her way for only a moment. His clarion was clearer now. The early-October air vibrated with it.

She found a service road and packed dirt on the far side of the meadow. It meandered into a windbreak of trees. Charlie's booted feet followed it into the grove. She lifted her face to the breeze as it rustled the gold, brown, and red leaves canopying her path and crunching softly beneath her feet. The music of chattering birds drifted down over the lane as shadows flitted in tempo with the swaying branches. It was a day for lazy walks and daydreaming. It was a world without the pressure of the newsroom. There were no deadlines, no emergencies, no disasters.

The stallion's shrill call cut through her reverie. She had reached her destination: the stallion's covert.

There had been no hint of a paddock from the road. The trees successfully blocked it from view. Not an easy task, for it was large with a slight rolling drop toward the south end. The inevitable five-foot white rail fencing surrounded it. From within the still, green paddock, the stallion appraised her warily.

Waiting silently just within the small copse, Charlie stared in awe at the vital male animal before her. He was still young, just a colt, but fully developed. The chestnut tone of his hide rippled in reflected glory in the sun. Carefully bred lines of chest, rump, and leg were accentuated by his alert stance. His nostrils flared as the wind carried her scent to him afresh. He snorted once and turned to race to the far side of the enclosure, his dark mane whipping into a halo around flattened ears. The gallop defined his racing bloodlines. His speed over the short distance exhilarated Charlie. At the far boundary, the chestnut did an about-face and sped back toward her, his hooves thundering on the turf.

Charlie climbed the fence to perch on the top rung while she watched his display.

The MacCrimmon Stables were well known for the quality of their thoroughbreds. The stud was highly rated and highly priced. She had covered a horse auction once with her television cameras and been astonished at the money bid for the colts and fillies on the block. Yet those same horses, when brought to the starting gates at race tracks around the world, brought home a small fortune in purses. The only disappointment in racing circles had been the lack of a Derby winner wearing the MacCrimmon tartan colors.

The chestnut had taken her measure by now. He ventured nearer the fence where she sat.

"You are a beauty, aren't you, fella," she cooed.

The horse snorted and tossed his head as if agreeing with her.

"Think so, do you?" Charlie grinned happily. "Quite a ladies' man? And fast. You'll show them your heels at the track or I miss my bet."

He answered her with a whinny and took a step closer, stretching his neck to sniff her knee.

Charlie didn't move. Her soft voice continued to praise him, assuring him she meant no harm. He moved closer, his nostrils blowing gently against her hand.

Suddenly his head came up and, wheeling, he pranced away.

"Oh, don't go, beauty," she cried after him.

The voice behind her was startling and harsh. "Can't you read?" it growled.

Charlie retained her grip on the fence and turned to the speaker angrily. "You scared him," she accused.

The man on horseback glared at her from beneath thick black brows. From his tanned skin she could guess that he spent a lot of time outdoors, not to mention the weather-beaten leather jacket he wore over a black plaid shirt. His legs were powerful as they straddled the large gray gelding. She had to admire the way he sat on a horse.

There was a calculating look in his eyes as he urged the horse closer and appraised her in an insolent manner. His forward-tilted, low-crowned gray Stetson couldn't hide the way he surveyed her breasts and hips before returning his furious dark gaze to her face. "This is private property. You're trespassing, sweetheart."

The wind tossed her short curls, causing tendrils to stretch across her pert nose. She pushed them back and lifted her chin defiantly. "Sorry to disappoint you, but I have the owner's permission." A half-truth at best, she admitted to herself. This man didn't know she hadn't met the actual owner yet, Mark MacCrimmon. She would brazen it out.

A surprised look came into his coal-black eyes. "The laird himself?" he asked.

"Yes, the laird himself," she braved. This decidely attractive ruffian wasn't going to get the better of her!

An infinitesimal touch of his heel urged the gray closer to the fence. The horse's head brushed against her. She could feel its damp, warm muzzle as yellow teeth nipped playfully at her sweater. The gelding snorted as the wool tickled his nostrils. Startled, Charlie lost her firm grip on the fence.

The man smiled mirthlessly at her. His lips stretched in a wolfish grimace. "And does the laird know where you are now, sweetheart?" he murmured.

16

"Of course he does," she blustered. "He won't appreciate hearing how you have harassed me."

The gray's head nuzzled her roughly again. "Wouldn't want a thing like that happening, would we?" he drawled. "He'd want me to treat a lady as she deserves."

Before Charlie realized his intention, she was swept from her precarious perch on the fence into his arms and seated sidesaddle before him. She was enveloped in the aroma of fine leather mingled with the scents of horses and his sweat. It made her acutely aware of the warmth of his arm about her waist, and of the strength of his thighs beneath his jeans. A five o'clock shadow accented the cruel set of his squared jaw. His jet eyes bored into her, ruthlessly sweeping away her bravado, peeling away the cool exterior she had maintained since her divorce.

His gaze dropped to her lips, drawn there against his will. How many nights had he watched her on the late newscast, watched her soft mouth curve invitingly, watched that delectable dimple peep from her cheek?

"What do you think you are doing?" she demanded as his face loomed near hers. She pulled back in an effort to put distance between herself and this dangerous man.

"Escorting you back to your car, ma'am," he said. The statement was a mockery. The gray stood sedate, belying his words. His arm tightened, pulling her closer so that her hands were wedged against the soft leather of his jacket. Her strength was moth-like compared to his. His large, leather-gloved hand caressed her jawline. "You never know what dangers await a lady alone."

Charlie's eyes burned with indignation, yet she found the temptation to look at his lips unbearable. The man exuded the same male animal magnetism that the young horse in the paddock possessed.

"If you don't let me go this instant . . ." she began.

His lips stretched to reveal perfect white teeth. "You'll

scream?" She felt his arms tighten at her waist. His lips curved in amusement.

Her eyes widened, reminding him of the autumn sky, endlessly blue, guileless. He found himself lost in them, drawn into them. Her breathing was shallow as her lips parted. Against his will, the man found himself accepting her unconscious invitation.

Charlie stiffened as his mouth claimed hers. His kiss was gentle at first, tentative. He drew back. His eyes locked with hers, reading a response in the azure depths.

Damn, he swore to himself. How could she look so vulnerable, so innocent? And taste of heaven.

Charlie swayed toward him in the saddle and he reclaimed her lips, ruthlessly now, determined to teach her a lesson. He thought.

Blood pounded in Charlie's temples. No man had kissed her this way since her marriage to Phil. She couldn't remember feeling so totally invaded, possessed, even by her husband. This stranger ravaged her emotions with his presence, his touch. He stroked her back, pressing her closer till she could feel the steady beat of his heart. Her own pulse hammered loudly in her ears, drowning out the song of the birds, the rustling trees, the irritated snorting of the young stallion. It decimated her reason. She knew she should fight him but found her lips responding, opening under his of their own volition.

He tasted, teased, and consumed her with the kiss. A burst of forgotten desire swept her as his hand intimately fondled her upper thigh. Her hands now gripped his shirt front as she returned the fire of his touch, sought the dancing flame he kindled. When the kiss ended, Charlie was shaken. Desperate, she sought a more familiar front, one of indignation at his assault. The fires banked momentarily as she surveyed the stranger.

"Are you quite through?" She was relieved to hear the icy

tone of her own voice. It was steady, strong. It didn't reveal her vulnerability.

He was not deceived. He smirked knowingly at her. "For now."

He knew she had responded to the kiss, that her cool exterior fought hard to conceal the pounding of her heart, and the furious racing of her blood. Color rose to her face. And so did her temper. The emotion stirred by him turned quickly to fury. Her turbulent eyes narrowed, glaring at him.

"Wasn't so bad, was it?" he said.

"For you perhaps. Don't think I won't report this . . . this . . ."

"Familiarity?"

"Mauling," she spat," to your employer."

His smile infuriated her. "The laird himself?"

"Yes."

He tightened his arm about her once again, pulling her supple body closer to his in the saddle. She stiffened momentarily. As he put the complacent gray in motion, she relaxed, moving with the horse's gait.

"Why waste a moment?" His breath was warm against her ear. "The sooner you report it, the better you will feel," the horseman declared cheerfully.

Charlie was silenced by impotent rage. How dare this man take liberties with her person and be so unconcerned about the consequences of his actions? She would certainly see that he was reprimanded or, better yet, fired for his actions.

The distance to her car was traveled quickly. The man's arm burned where it touched her waist. She wished she could bank the fires he aroused, feelings that had lain dormant for so many years. The knowledge of their rebirth hammered at her senses.

He swung to the ground in one graceful movement and lifted her from the saddle. His strong, large hands encircled her small waist, letting her slide slowly along the length of his hard, lean body. She was fully aware of his desire and half afraid of the answering quickness in her own breath.

Charlie clenched her fists at her sides. "You . . . you . . ." she sputtered.

He drew back, leering. "My regards to the laird." He leaped into the saddle again and turned the gray. With an arrogant tip of his hat, he touched the gelding's side with his heel, sending him into a gallop.

Angrily, Charlie kicked at a tuft of late wildflowers along the side of the road. The man and horse were one as they covered the distance to the top of the pasture and disappeared into the grove. He was a centaur, muscle and limb part of the gray who responded to his thoughts, it seemed, more than the light touch of his heel and hands. Hands that were strong, knowing, and possessed erotic knowledge.

She climbed into the Impulse and slammed the door. Damn him. When she met the owner of MacCrimmon Stables this evening she would certainly tell him . . .

Charlie smacked her hand flat against the steering wheel. Hell! She didn't even know the horseman's name.

From within the copse, man and horse watched the sleek red car speed down the lane. He leaned casually against the saddle horn, unconsciously mimicking the pose of frontier scouts in a myriad of paintings.

His thoughts were on the young woman long after her sports car was lost to view. Only the dust hanging in the air betrayed her passage through the quiet pastures.

Behind him the young stallion whinnied for attention. The gray answered of its own accord, moving with an easy gait to the fence. The man scratched the young horse's red-brown coat. The chestnut snorted and edged closer. Lumps of sugar found their way from the man's jacket to the colt's questing muzzle.

"Yes, I know, Pride," he told the two-year-old. "I acted like a damn bastard. I wonder why?" His face turned toward the now vacant road. "She's far more desirable in person."

The horse nuzzled his hand. "It should certainly make dinner interesting this evening," the man said, turning back to the colt and rubbing the damp nose vigorously. A sardonic smile curved his fine lips before he pulled his hat lower over his eyes and cantered off. "Very interesting indeed."

Chapter Two

DESPITE THE MODERN comforts of her room, Charlie found it difficult to relax when she returned to MacCrimmon Manor. She was still shaken by her encounter with the horseman. It wasn't so much his actions as her own reactions that she found disturbing.

His methods of dealing with an impertinent trespasser had been unorthodox, but he had just been doing his job.

Now that his irritating smirk was out of sight, her temper cooled. On second thought, Charlie decided not to mention the episode to MacCrimmon when she met him. She was at the estate to do a story, not to make trouble for the staff.

It was ridiculous to let her own unease over the network proposition color her reactions to things and events. She hadn't been attracted to the horseman, she told herself sternly. She had been startled, overcome by his superior strength, astonished at his actions. That was all. If she imagined anything more had occurred, she might as well admit to a belief in ghosts!

There was something about MacCrimmon Manor that lent itself to such a belief. Although the main hall, with its medieval grandeur undiminished, seemed to cater to the superstition, the decor of the rest of the house was modern.

Yet the eerie sensation that other eyes watched her movements persisted.

Charlie shrugged off the feeling and turned her thoughts to her assignment.

The black tassels of the woman's silk shawl quivered then danced as she punctuated her words with her hands. "But, of course, the reasons many manifestations appear are based in family legends," she insisted. "For instance, the apparition that walks Balmoral Castle . . ."

Jack Donahue leaned forward from the deeply cushioned couch. "Now, wait a minute. Shouldn't we concentrate on sightings in the States? What connection do English spooks have with the ghosts here at MacCrimmon?"

Charlie Arden paused in the doorway to enjoy the grimaces the unknown woman made at Jack's derogatory words.

"Spooks! Ghosts!" she sputtered before regaining control. The fringe jumped as she expounded. "We prefer more scientific designations—ectoplasm or apparition or phantasms—when dealing with manifestations."

"Same difference," Jack insisted with a grin calculated to irritate.

Charlie smiled softly. This was the same man who had filled the station van with cameras, determined to produce a picture of a ghost. Now he sounded like a hardened skeptic.

The room was a comfortable, warm blend of old and new. The darkly paneled walls decorated with framed prints of horses gave Charlie the impression that she had stepped back in time. Not to a feudal age, which was the feeling she had experienced in the main hall with its display of medieval weapons, but back a mere hundred years to a comfortable Victorian country estate. The plush carpet and modular sofa were of 20th-century design and a rich green shade, reminiscent of a lush forest. The lighting was muted, adding to the intimate atmosphere, leaving many corners draped in shadows. The furniture was grouped to face the massive fireplace, the focal point of the room. Flames licked at split cedar logs within its wide, yawning mouth.

Charlie inhaled the fragrant scent of the burning wood and turned her attention to the five people gathered around the fireplace.

The expressive shawl belonged to a spare, pallid-complexed woman dressed in black satin. Creases fanned away from the corners of her ever-moving eyes, as they flickered eagerly from one speaker to another. Next to Jack sat an elegant blonde. The firelight cast a warm glow over her high cheekbones. She appeared to be amused by the conversation, as if she guessed Jack's intention. Other than to be the center of attention, Charlie doubted if he had one.

An older, bearded man with sandy hair sat in solitary splendor. He stared into the tumbler between his large hands as if the talk of apparitions bored him.

A younger man straddled a hassock. He seemed vaguely familiar, his looks dark and handsome, but Charlie was sure she had never met him.

The older man gave up contemplation of his nearly empty glass and caught sight of Charlie in the entranceway. He rose to his feet, smiling a welcome.

"Miss Arden," the younger man greeted. He crossed the room to her side with long strides. "I'm so pleased to see you at MacCrimmon," he said.

He was very handsome, Charlie found. His dark turtle-neck and camel's-hair sports coat were dramatic. The crease in his dark wool trousers was razor sharp. Blue highlights danced in his carefully styled black hair. "I'm Don Mac-Crimmon," he said.

Charlie returned his handshake and allowed him to draw her nearer the fire. "This is my cousin Gwen Hale," he said of the elegant blond. The woman nodded languidly, her smile still one of amusement rather than welcome.

Donald MacCrimmon was already turning to the older man. "Our head trainer, Tim Tierney," he introduced.

Tierney held out his hand to Charlie. His grip was strong, warm. "Welcome to MacCrimmon, Miss Arden. It's nice to see such an attractive new face around here."

"Thank you, Mr. Tierney. I hope everyone will still feel that way once Jack and I have strung out all our cameras."

"Ah, yes, the ghosts," the older man said. Charlie expected his broad face to crease in amusement. It didn't.

"Don't let Miss Rinehart hear you call them that," Don cautioned. "She takes exception to the term."

Tierney finished his drink. "Ghosts are ghosts, Don. Since we're the ones who live with them we ought to be able to call them as we see them."

"See them?" Charlie echoed. "You've actually seen them?"

The trainer shrugged. "Yes and no. I've *felt* them rather than seen them."

"Felt," Charlie mused. "The cold clammy hand at the back of your neck, the sensation of evil?" She smiled suddenly. "I'm afraid my whole experience with ghostly phenomena is in the movies."

"The kind that deserve the term *chillers?*" Don asked with a grin.

The atmosphere lightened as Tierney laughed. "I believe Miss Arden is a skeptic," Don said. He turned to the older man with an amused look. "Like you once were, Tim."

"Oh, I still am to a great extent. It isn't something a rational person accepts on faith."

"That gives it a rather religious lean, doesn't it, Mr. Tierney?" Charlie asked.

"Classifying ghosts, or perhaps I should say spirits, along with faith healers? Or with life after death? That I do believe in, Miss Arden. And it is just as undocumented by scientists. Impossibly so, in fact," Tierney continued.

Charlie found herself liking Tim Tierney very much. His

tone had been that of a businessman not a believer. He recognized facts. Donald MacCrimmon, the man, was attractive but she was wary of all politicians. Gwen had been helpful in arranging to have the news team at the manor. Could that be construed as too helpful? And what of the head of the family, Mark MacCrimmon? She was anxious to meet the man behind the continued success of the MacCrimmon Stables. Stan Powers had set quite a challenge with the ghost hunt assignment, but she knew there were other stories to milk during her stay in the manor. There were many angles to use on the MacCrimmon clan. Sports, fashion, society, politics . . . and definitely a story about a man his employees called *the laird*. Even the horseman at the paddock had referred to MacCrimmon by the feudal Scottish title.

Just the thought of the horseman's stormy eyes made her heart leap. Charlie forced the picture from her mind. As she had dressed for dinner, the episode at the paddock had replayed in her mind much too often. She had found herself staring blankly into the mirror seeing the harshly drawn brows and powerful physique of the insolent man as he sat at his ease on the broad back of his gray gelding.

Donald MacCrimmon nodded at her. "Perhaps Miss Rinehart can answer some of your questions," he said. "She is our expert in residence currently." He nodded toward the woman seated near Jack. "Katrine Rinehart, Charlie Arden. Kat's a medium."

The fringed shawl fluttered as Katrine acknowledged the introduction. "You are much lovelier in person than on television," she said. "Your aura is much clearer."

Charlie exchanged a quick look with Jack. His eyes sparkled, answering hers. If there were anyone in the room capable of hoodwinking the Channel 5 crew, Katrine Rinehart was it. She seemed to have *charlatan* written in glowing letters all over her. It would be interesting, Charlie decided, to discover who had hired this particular psychic medium.

"Thank you, Miss Rinehart," she said and took a seat on a hassock near the medium.

"Oh, I'm Kat to everyone," the woman gushed. She threw a melting smile Don's way.

Gwen stretched with feline grace. "Since we will all be working rather closely together, I'm sure it would be far more comfortable using first names." She grinned. "There is something about our ghosts that calls for informality."

"Just how many spirits do you have haunting MacCrimmon, Gwen?" Charlie inquired.

Gwen smoothed an errant blond curl back from her forehead. "We should have a visit from Lord Claymore soon, but right now the most active spirit is Mary MacCrimmon Douglas."

"Don't forget Angus," Tim contributed. He looked at his empty tumbler. "We could do without Angus. I'd rather drink his spirits than encounter his ghost. Bartender! Another of the same. What will you have, Miss Arden?"

She requested a white wine, which Tierney relayed toward one of the many dark corners of the room. She saw a shadowy male figure bend to retrieve a bottle from below the bar counter.

"Angus was the laird's and Don's father," Gwen explained.

"He had the misfortune to break his neck in a fall a few years ago, didn't he? Why would his . . ." Charlie paused and glanced at the medium.

"Essence," the woman breathed.

"Essence then, be earth-bound?"

Katrine Rinehart beamed. "Quite the proper term. Many times the entity lingers at the scene of its death, refusing to admit life's essence has been drained."

"Really?" Charlie fought the quiver of her lip. The woman could not be serious. Her whole manner was extremely theatrical. Perhaps if she had been older, the act would have been believable.

"That's nonsense. Angus knows he's dead," Tierney said.

"Ah," Kat sighed romantically. "Unable to release his loved ones."

Gwen and Don exchanged a grin. "Let's change that to first-born. He haunts Mark," Don said.

The medium looked disconcerted for a moment before she recovered. "The new laird. Yes, yes. Your father is unable to release the reins of authority to his successor."

"Not Angus," Gwen said. "Mark ran things long before the accident."

"An urgent matter concerning the family often brings the loved one across the veil from the other side," Katrine insisted.

Her audience was not receptive. They laughed. "Angus never cared for any but his hoofed family," Tierney said. "Oh, he loved his wife and boys, he just gave all his attention and energies to breeding horses."

From his reclining position against the cushions, Jack's lazy voice suggested, "Why not ask him why he's hanging around?"

"Yes," the medium breathed. "A seance. The atmosphere here is conducive to contact with the departed."

Charlie's lips twitched again.

Across the room, behind the bar, the man admired the redheaded newswoman's manner. He caught the slight upturn of her lovely lips before she controlled the impulse. He sympathized with her. Katrine Rinehart had forced her way into the manor with a letter of introduction from Gwen's mother. A very forceful woman, Imogene MacCrimmon Hale refused to recognize any ruling of his when it came to the FAMILY. Imogene always gave it a full measure of capitals in her letters. Recalling the one that had found its way from her preferred home in London to his desk, the man grimaced. Imogene raved about the results Katrine Rinehart had in contacting Boyden, Gwen's elder brother, drowned in a boating accident. The letter had simply told him that Kat Rinehart would be arriving to quell the ghostly uproar.

The psychic medium's arrival had been just the first instance of Imogene's meddling. At a cocktail party she had buttonholed a network executive from North American Broadcasting. Things had snowballed beyond Imogene's wildest hopes after that. The executive had liked the idea of catching a ghost on film. He took the idea to a meeting where the project was given the okay, providing expenses could be kept to a minimum. Perhaps with a local crew? That was when Louisville's Channel 5 news team had entered the scene.

Charlie Arden's investigation of those same ancestral shades should have irritated him just as much as the idea of a psychic medium in his home had earlier. But now that she was actually at the manor, he found he was pleased. She wasn't aware of his presence. It allowed him ample opportunity to study her as the group discussed the hauntings. The firelight enhanced the amber glow in the auburn curls of her hair. It outlined her slim figure, her breasts, narrow waist, gently rounded hips, her long, shapely legs. He remembered the womanly smell of her, the soft feel of her in his arms, the fight quickly consumed in fire as she responded to his kiss.

She turned to smile at Don. It was the same sweet smile she gave to the news cameras every evening, but the watching man experienced a tightening of his jaw muscles. She would not smile at him that way, he knew. Then again, perhaps she would. After all, he mused as he picked up the crystal goblet of wine, she didn't know who he was yet. Her reaction would be amusing.

"No seances before dinner, I beg," Tierney said in a pained voice, having listened to Kat Rinehart tell of her past successes for the last few minutes.

"Besides, our cameras should be set up for such a big event," Charlie declared.

A delicate glass of wine appeared at her elbow. "White wine for the lady," a familiar male voice said behind her. His footsteps had been hushed by the deep pile carpet.

Charlie whirled to find the handsome face of the man she had been trying to put from her mind. His freshly shaven jawline was squared and drew her gaze to his lips against her will. His dark brow rose sardonically as her eyes widened in surprise.

"Thanks, old man," Don said. "Don't think you've had the pleasure of meeting our guests. Charlie Arden, my brother Mark."

His jet eyes danced as he turned and smiled crookedly at her. "Mark MacCrimmon, laird of this humble abode," he said.

Don introduced Jack while Charlie recovered her wits. The laird, the owner of MacCrimmon Stables, the maddening man from the paddock, all the same! Jack was shaking hands with him, laughing at some comment she hadn't caught. All she saw were Mark's broad shoulders encased in a gray Harris tweed jacket. His white silk shirt was casually open at the neck. He towered over the other men, radiating confidence and authority. Knowing who he was now, she marveled that she hadn't known him immediately. The other men were pale by comparison.

Mark turned back to her and noted with pleasure the heightened color in her cheeks. "I hope you enjoy your stay at MacCrimmon, Miss Arden. If there are any annoyances, I hope you will let me know."

She forced a smile and met the challenge in his eyes. "Thank you, Mr. MacCrimmon. I hope you won't find our cameras irritating. Am I right in assuming you are not in favor of my investigation?"

Don laughed. "Charlie doesn't waste any time, does she? Pinned you right away, Mark."

"I find it a pleasure, Miss Arden," the laird said smoothly.

His eyes flicked over her. "I'm looking forward to your investigation."

His words and manner were far from sarcastic, but Charlie perceived the double meanings. If he was throwing the gauntlet, she would accept. There was no going back, after all. She could apologize, but there was something in his look that told her he would still antagonize her with the memory of what had passed between them that afternoon. Shoulders squared, head cocked to one side, she measured him. "You wouldn't mind working closely with me on some aspects, Mr. MacCrimmon?"

Mark grinned. She had spunk, this delicious little redhead. He admired the way she had recognized his challenge and joined battle. "I assure you, I would enjoy it very much, Charlie," he said. A soft Scots burr caressed her name, rolling the *R*.

She felt his eyes linger on her face, studying each feature. He would offer no apology for his earlier behavior. On the contrary, there was a promise of a repeat performance. Her heart beat faster at the thought, although whether in fear or excitement, she wasn't sure. Her professional ethics forbidding mixing business with pleasure were based in her desire to avoid all emotional commitments. Why was it this man caused her to forget her hurt, her fear of getting involved? She should be furious with him for deceiving her earlier, for causing the barriers she had spent years building to crack and threaten to topple. Instead she found herself smiling at him.

"Was I mistaken, Mr. MacCrimmon? I thought this clan had forsaken the Highlands."

"The Highlands, yes, but not the romance of the Gaelic."

"Ah," sighed Kat Rinehart. "The romance of Bonnie Prince Charlie and the Highland clans will live forever." Her elaborate tower of curls tipped in Mark's direction. Her wide smile was for him alone. She scuttled over to make room on the sofa next to her, rustling the full skirt of her black dress as she swept it out of his way.

Mark chose to perch on the arm of the sofa near his cousin Gwen. "Are you an advocate of the Stuart Prince, Kat?"

"Such a disastrous young man," she said mournfully.

Charlie wondered briefly if the emotion was for the long dead Charles Stuart or over Mark's choice of seating.

"I was one of a group that tried to contact him once," the medium continued. "But he had already departed to a higher plane."

"A what?" Jack demanded.

"The spirit levels," Mark explained. "Like stages of evolution only in this case, levels of consciousness."

Kat beamed. "I had no idea you were so knowledgeable, Mark!"

Don chuckled. "We grew up around ghosts, remember? I think each one of us did a school paper on them at one time or another."

"No, I borrowed yours and Mark's," Gwen said with a tender smile. "I just retyped them with my name."

Charlie sipped at her wine and surveyed the MacCrimmon cousins gravely. "I suppose you are all rather familiar with the phenomena then."

"Ask away," Don offered. His hand waved in Gwen's direction then Mark's. "What we three don't know, I'm sure Kat can fill in."

"I think what Charlie is thinking is that we are up to all the tricks. Have ghost, will produce," Mark said levelly. "You'll just have to take our word that any phantoms your cameras or you personally encounter are not constructed in a workshop."

"What about induced hallucinations?" Charlie prompted.

"Induced? Hypnotism or drugs?" Mark's smile was evil. "You do have it in for us, Miss Arden."

Gwen got to her feet in one fluid motion. "Perhaps we

need someone with a different point of view. The appearances have increased of late, and I for one would like to know why. But if I'm not mistaken, that is Mrs. M at the door to announce dinner."

"Why not call for an exorcism if the disturbances are disruptive?" Charlie asked Don.

He looked surprised to hear such a suggestion. "They're family," he said. "We don't want them gone, just quieted."

"And a news team is supposed to accomplish that?" she asked, unbelieving.

Jack brushed against her arm as he moved to follow Gwen from the room. "Why not?" he whispered. "You think La Rinehart could?"

Don heard and laughed. "Let's say we have all the bases covered."

"Why not a parapsychologist then? They would be far more qualified then we are," she persisted.

"Yes, Don," Mark said. "Are we to expect another guest?"

The younger man looked irritated. "I haven't found one willing to rush to our assistance, Mark. Gwen is still working on it."

The laird smiled. "Doesn't that ease your mind, Charlie?" He took her arm, steering her toward the dining room door. His touch seemed to burn her. "Now, tell me all you know about the spirit world. We've got to find a way to stump you. I suppose a sheet on a wire is out?" he asked playfully.

She smiled at the outrageous suggestion. "Yes, I think so. Perhaps dry ice for ghostly vapors?"

"Excellent, but still rather tame. I think better on a full stomach though." His eyes met hers as she looked up into his face briefly. He felt he was gazing into deep blue pools. If only they had met under different circumstances. Or he hadn't made an ass of himself in the meadow. After hearing Pride's call he had over-reacted to her presence. The colt had obviously accepted her though.

Mark dropped the bantering tone. "No matter what I could concoct, believe me, Charlie, it wouldn't come close to the real thing. I don't think you'll be disappointed at all."

"No, I don't think I will be," she murmured, but at that moment she wasn't thinking of the ghostly inhabitants of the manor. She was thinking of the master, MacCrimmon himself.

Charlie felt manipulated. She had tried to turn the conversation at dinner toward the upcoming political campaign. Her ventures were stifled by the laird who turned the conversation to the MacCrimmon ghosts.

Mark had seated her on his right. Under his eye, she felt. The effervescent Kat Rinehart was on his left. The medium turned often, as if puzzled, to the vacant chair, the hostess chair, at the foot of the table. Since Kat gave Mark her most dazzling smiles, Charlie construed the woman's behavior as ambition to fill the position herself.

The dining room was a continuation of the lounge. But here the atmosphere had been lightened by the addition of double glass doors leading to the terrace. The long table stood on an island patch of Persian rug that appeared to float on the sea of green carpet. Delicate bone china and Waterford crystal goblets picked up the warm glow from lighted candles in gleaming silver candelabras. The candles were for atmosphere only, Charlie realized, for each of the paintings along the walls was highlighted by electric lights.

The meal itself was moderate. A standing rib of beef sat on a sideboard where Mrs. MacLynn, the housekeeper, supervised each plate before a neatly dressed maid returned it to the table. No wine glass was allowed to remain empty.

It was the nearness of her host that occupied Charlie's innermost thoughts though. It became an effort to remember she had a job to do and a multitude of questions to ask. She wasn't a dream-struck schoolgirl anymore. Phil had killed that part of her long ago. Logic had dictated she build walls. The fact that no one had managed to scale the barriers, though many had tried, had not disturbed her before. The kisses Mark had stolen at the paddock should have left her unshaken. They hadn't. The walls hadn't fallen but she had the feeling Mark MacCrimmon had gotten inside them already. It would take a determined effort on her part to repulse the effects of his assault. She was a professional reporter on assignment. She could and would put her physical attraction to the man from her mind. That's all it was, after all. There was a job to do. And the job wasn't restricted to a ghost hunt even if that was the story she had to hand in at the end of her stay. A reporter's career could boom with an inside on politics. She certainly didn't intend to have all her eggs in a ghostly basket.

Unconsciously Charlie squared her shoulders and opened fire. "I understand you are thinking of running for public office, Don. Which seat are you after?"

The question startled a bark of laughter from Don. "No comment, Miss Arden. Believe me, you will be the first to know among our friends in the press."

She opened her mouth to press the question when Mark interrupted. "Feel honored, Charlie. You have an exclusive. The trip won't be a total waste."

She blinked. Had he read her mind?

Mark turned his attention to his brother, continuing the bantering tone. "The wording sounds right, pal, but you really must work on the sincerity. By the way, do you expect me to vote for you?"

"I appreciate the future interview," Charlie said lightly in an effort to bring the conversation back to Don's plans. She dared not look toward the man on her left. He had the power to strip her hard-won composure. It was all she had to cling to in his presence. "The near future, I hope, Don. Tomorrow?"

"I'm sure it will be the very near future, bonny Charlie," Mark interjected. He took a sip of wine. His dark eyes were warm as they rested on her face. "You'll want to give everyone the third degree on our hauntings, won't you? Tomorrow sounds soon enough to start."

Charlie clenched her teeth. Her smile was a little fine as she faced her host. "It will have to be, won't it? I am on a deadline."

Katrine Rinehart leaned forward eagerly. "I personally find a plural manifestation fascinating. Have you experienced a materialization of ectoplasm personally, Mark?"

He leaned back in the comfortable armchair, his elbows on the arms, his fingertips together. "A ghost, you mean, Kat?" he asked.

Charlie breathed a sigh of relief as his attention was directed away from her. His interference in the conversation made concentration difficult. The sooner she and MacCrimmon got things on a professional basis, the better. Even if he refused to accept it, she would apologize for trespassing. Hopefully that would put an end to the tension between them and she would be able to concentrate only on this assignment.

Despite the medium's earlier insistence on scientific terms, she conceded Mark's use of the word *ghost* with a flirtatious grin. "Yes, ghosts. I have never witnessed a manifestation. Being a medium, the spirits speak through me, of course, while I am in a trance."

Jack's knee nudged Charlie's under the table. "So actually seeing a ghost is a fantasy of yours, Kat?" he asked.

There was security in the camaraderie she and Jack shared, a sense of story when they worked. It was a kinship that recognized the other's right to privacy away from the job. Gratefully, she picked up his intent and enlarged on the theme. "It seems a shame that in your profession you never see what you are dealing with," Charlie agreed. "I do hope you will allow us to film your seance. Let's hope it proves interesting for all concerned." It was clear invitation for the woman to put on a show for the news team. A manifestation would surely materialize. A manufactured manifestation. No matter what Mark said, she felt someone in the manor was preparing a publicity hoax.

"We have a large selection for you to choose from," Mark said lightly. "They came with the manor."

His was a rich baritone, the kind of male voice she loved. It had an announcer's quality, authoritative yet comforting. It would sound well on the tape. Or perhaps she would be wiser to steer clear of Mark MacCrimmon. It was a thought worth pursuing.

"Some nights you'd swear we were having a masquerade, there are so many centuries represented," Gwen said.

"All at once?" Jack demanded.

"Not usually," she assured him. "They do have anniversaries. You can almost guarantee an appearance those nights."

Charlie found her mind wandering. What was the matter with her? Her awareness of her host was distracting. She had to stay on track with this story. Charlie leaned forward, reentering the conversation. "I don't suppose one of those anniversaries is within the next few days?"

"Funny you should ask," Mark said. Charlie glanced at his dark, attractive face but he directed her attention down the table to Gwen.

"We rather planned your invitation around Lord Claymore's walk," the blonde admitted. "If you remember your history, in April of 1746, Bonny Prince Charlie and his Scots were defeated on Culloden Moor. The manor was in the Highlands then, of course, in a quiet valley quite cut off from the rest of the world."

"Claymore had married the daughter of the house. His finances weren't in very healthy condition and he had persuaded the laird to part with the girl's dowry before the wedding. He stood behind the Stuart claim totally when it came to financing the bid for the crown," Don added.

"He wasn't one to jeopardize his person, though. He stayed at MacCrimmon with his bride while the laird and his eldest sons followed the prince," Gwen said. "They were all lost in the massacre at Culloden.

"Claymore took the defeat harder than most of the prince's supporters. He sank into a deep moody state and became a hermit, remaining in his room for months. Before winter set in he was dead, leaving the MacCrimmon women and the young schoolboy laird to fend for themselves."

"You can depend on Claymore now," Gwen said. "I've never known him to miss his walk."

"He's due to appear Friday night," Don added.

Jack looked around the table. "All right," he said. "I'll bite. What's he going to do? Pace his old room?"

It was Mark who answered. His voice took on an eerie quality in the stillness of the candle-lit room. "Claymore walks down the main staircase," he said and paused. Charlie was sure it was for effect but found herself holding her breath all the same. "Then he falls on his sword."

Chapter Three

JACK SPRAWLED ON the love seat in Charlie's room, one leg thrown over the arm. He peered at her through the lens of a hand-held camera, adjusting it for close-ups and back again to take in her lithe form curled in the matching chair across from him.

Absorbed in thought, Charlie was hardly aware of his presence. The light from the warming fireplace flickered over the pale curve of her cheek, exposing a profile of dark lashes and up-tilted nose. The coffee-colored turtleneck and corduroy jeans she'd changed into blended with the shadows.

He adjusted the lens and snapped a picture.

The slight sound of the shutter roused her from her reverie. "Thinking of setting up a studio again, Jack?"

He zoomed in to catch the unusual shadow accentuating her features. "Still have that showing of my work in mind. You haven't forgotten it, I'm sure."

"Hardly," she said. "From all the photographs of me you've taken over the last few years, I'm the star attraction."

"A beautiful woman always attracts a crowd. They'll think I'm brilliant by gazing at your lovely face."

"Ha!" Her laugh was brittle. "You should take more shots of that gorgeous wife of yours. How's Ginny taking your staying out here?"

"Okay," he said, familiar with the way she evaded looking him in the eye. Something was up. "We go back a long way, Chuck."

Her features softened, but the closed expression remained. "Yes, we do, Jack. We have a lot of wonderful memories."

"So?" he prompted.

"So, what?"

"The brooding. What's the matter?" The camera continued to hide his face. The focus changed, and every so often she heard the whirling click as he added still another study of her face to his collection.

She had been reviewing the evening in her mind, finding that each gesture, every look and word of Mark's had been recorded with unnerving clarity in her memory. It wasn't an affliction she felt comfortable exposing. Even to her best friend, which Jack undoubtedly was. "It's the assignment," she said, side-stepping the real issue. "I can't get a grip on it."

Jack nodded. "Yeah. They're a weird bunch."

Her turquoise eyes sparked defensively. "What do you mean, weird?"

"Believing in ghosts. Or thinking they can convince us that they do."

"Oh," she said and settled back in the chair. "Well, it will take some doing to convince me. What do you know about spirit photography?"

He shrugged. "I'm sure I could doctor photographs to get some fairly convincing spooks."

Her red curls bounced as she shook her head. "No, I mean historically. I *know* you're a whiz in the darkroom."

He chose to misunderstand her. "All hearsay, Chuck. You've never had the courage to go into a darkroom with me." He leered theatrically at her over the camera.

Charlie ignored the lighthearted comment. "I did some

checking at the library yesterday after Stan dropped this bomb in my lap. Seems spirit photos have been around ever since the beginning of photography. In 1848 the spirit field really came into its own in the U.S. A couple of sisters made contact with the dearly departed by way of knocks. It knocked the gullible Victorians on both sides of the Atlantic off their feet. Americans were the biggest suckers. They swallowed it all. Hook, line, and sinker. Houdini spent a lot of time exposing fakes, too."

"Obviously that was before everyone started waiting for him to answer from the grave." Jack struggled to remain serious. "So you think the MacCrimmons are doctoring photos? Shall we launch a full-scale search of this mausoleum for a darkroom setup? Only three of them are capable. Maybe there's a secret passage."

Charlie finally succumbed to the levity in his voice. "I didn't think we'd have to deal with their pictures, dope." She grinned across at him. "Besides, you'd make a lousy sleuth with those size fourteens of yours."

Jack held up one foot and surveyed its length through the camera lens. "Okay, carry on, Chuck. They won't be supplyin' the pix."

Her almond-shaped eyes narrowed in thought. "It wouldn't take a darkroom to manifest something for *our* cameras though."

"And we do have three suspects, Sherlock," Jack murmured.

"Don could be trying to get extra publicity . . ."

"The goddess ditto," he said.

Charlie looked surprised. "The goddess? Gwen? Jack, I didn't know your interest lay in that quarter."

He studiously removed the completed roll of film from the camera. "And then there is the laird."

"I don't think he'd . . ."

"Just for the unholy glee of it," he interrupted her. "Don't put blinders on, Chuck. I'm not saying he's not a nice guy. You two have certainly hit it off."

He watched for a reaction. But Charlie was in control of her feelings at present. If he had expected to take her unaware with his statement, Jack was disappointed.

Charlie ignored his last comment. "I don't think you should discount the Rinehart woman. From what little I read yesterday, mediums, if indeed she is a true one, are rather unstable personalities. If they have any psychic ability, it is most likely a telepathy from the living, not the dead."

"Unstable, I'd believe. Or a frustrated and bad actress," he said.

"Whichever, she bears watching." Charlie twisted her legs into a lotus position. Her expression was thoughtful but her eyes were listless.

Jack reloaded the camera. "You haven't got a direction on this, do you, Chuck?"

Her lips twisted wryly. "You got it, partner. I'm lost. Any ideas?"

"You're asking me? I just take the pretty pictures."

"Well, we've got to start somewhere! What have they told us that we can get our teeth into?"

"Nuffin'," Jack said inelegantly.

"Damn. We need a parapsychologist to coordinate this."

"A what?"

"Parapsychologist. An expert on phenomena like ghosts. Don claims he's been trying to get one out here but hasn't succeeded yet. The question is, can they dig one up, or can we for that matter, and still make our deadline?" Her hand ran through her curls, raking them into attractive disarray.

Jack stifled a yawn. "It'll all jell, Chuck. Sleep on it. I've got cameras set up to take pictures on a time lapse so there might be something to go on tomorrow."

She sat straighter in surprise. "You do? Fantastic! Where?"

"In a ghost-infested place. It's good. Trust me." He settled down into the cushions and closed his eyes.

"Okay." Charlie's dimple peeped out as she eyed her camera man. "Are you planning on camping out here?"

Jack opened one eye. "It is a haunted house. Thought maybe you'd be afraid to be alone."

"Sure it's not the idea that your room was the scene of visitations?"

"Naw. Besides, Gwen did say no bones have rattled there in the last twenty years." Slowly he got to his feet and stretched. "If you're sure . . ."

She waved him from the room.

The silence was unearthly once the door closed behind Jack. The only sounds were those made by the fire as it blazed blue and orange, chasing shadows around the room.

Charlie leaned forward, elbow on knee, hand to cheek, staring at the dancing flames. Mark MacCrimmon had certainly been a different person at dinner. He was a thoughtful host. On the other hand, she had not been a considerate guest. Just the thought of their meeting and the passion of his kisses had raised her back.

If they had not met until evening, would the attraction have been as compelling? Would her reaction have been so violent?

For that matter, which man was the real Mark MacCrimmon—the ruffian she had met at the stallion's meadow, or the gentleman who had taken her in to dinner?

A soft knock on her door interrupted further thoughts. "Miss Arrrden?" came the housekeeper's quiet burr.

Charlie crossed the room quickly. "Mrs. MacLynn! Is something wrong?" she demanded, pulling the door open.

"Wrong?" the little wren echoed with a warm smile. "Now what could go wrong about here, lassie? Nay, 'tis the laird. He's wishful to see you."

Charlie was confused. A variety of emotions battled within her breast. He wanted to see her.

The housekeeper's grin widened happily. "His office is the front room on the ground floor, nearest the stables, miss. Can you find your way?"

Charlie's first reaction had been joy quickly replaced with a fear of a reprimand for straying past the *no trespassing* warnings earlier. A guarded expression replaced both emotions in quick succession. "Thank you, Mrs. MacLynn. Did he say what it was about?"

"Nay, lass, only that I be quick about it. Best you be as well." Her eyes twinkled. "The laird is used to getting his way. But I think he could wait while you fussed a bit."

Charlie's hand went to her tangled curls. "I'll try to be quick, Mrs. MacLynn," she said as the housekeeper turned away into the darkened hall.

She did more than run a comb through her hair. She applied a fresh coat of mascara and touched up her lipstick. Then, standing back from the full-length mirror on the closet doors, she pulled her sweater down over her hips to outline her figure.

The corridor was almost pitch black once she left the cozy comfort of her room. There was a dim light burning at the landing, but her steps were unsure until she reached it. A draft raced along the stone wall, sending a chill up her spine. All this talk of ghosts was going to affect her imagination as it had Jack's. She hadn't been deceived by his bravado. All she had to do was keep telling herself that MacCrimmon Manor wasn't haunted. It was just an old building and as such was prone to drafts, creaks, and moans that had nothing to do with the supernatural. There were no such things as ghosts.

All the same, she had the distinct feeling that she was not alone as she ran her hand along the wall as a guide and down the staircase to the main floor. The creaking of the stairs under her tread was eerie. It echoed in the cold, vast, medieval splendor of the entrance hall. The only illumination came from a desk lamp shining through the massive doorway to her left. It cast a scant, sinister light on the ancient museum pieces. Charlie repeated a litany. "There are no ghosts, there are no ghosts, no ghosts, no gho—"

She hadn't realized she was whispering it aloud until a deep voice from the shadows at the foot of the stairs asked, "There aren't? Who are you trying to convince?"

Charlie recoiled in surprise then relaxed. "Must you always sneak up on me!" she demanded, furious at being caught talking to herself. Her heart pounded, despite the relief to find the speaker was of the mortal rather than spiritual realm. Not for the world did she want him to know how her heart had vaulted to her throat in terror until she recognized his voice.

Mark's hands were raised in mock horror. "Pax! I'm sorry if I scared you. I thought you might have gotten lost and was going to find you."

Miffed, she turned and entered his office. "I wasn't scared, just startled. I'm a grown woman, after all."

"Of course," he mumbled. It irritated her to hear the amusement in his voice as he followed her into the room and shut the door with a decisive snap.

The office was extremely masculine. She was beginning to expect dark paneling. But the rich mahogany tone was so much a part of him that she felt the house was a reflection of Mark MacCrimmon rather than a feature of the historical building. In this room only three walls were covered by wood. A large, framed map hung on one wall. The legend *MacCrimmon* was scripted in a scrolled area at the lower right corner. If the scale could be judged by the sketched buildings, the area of the MacCrimmon property was enormous. Adjacent to the map a number of black, four-drawer file cabinets braced the wall on either side of the door. Still, it was the inner wall, to her right, that caught and held her attention. Stretching from floor to ceiling were glass display cases crowded with shining loving cups and trophies, bright ribbons and medals. Next to each award sat a small framed photograph of a horse and rider.

"I had no idea the tartan had swept up these," she said, indicating the entire case. "But why this empty section?"

"Need you ask, Charlie?" Mark reached past her, brushing against her shoulder, to tap the glass in the center of the case before the vacant shelves. "We've only the Derby to go."

"And the others?" she asked, motioning to the remaining shelves. They formed a triangular formation.

"Perhaps a couple other races?" His dark brow arched above his left eye.

"The Triple Crown?"

He nodded.

Her face lifted to his. "Is that why you were so abrupt this afternoon?"

Mark's face creased in amusement. "Is that what I was? Somehow I thought you'd use a stronger term."

Charlie turned away from him, troubled to be reminded of her rash statements earlier. She stared out over the lower set of shutters that covered each of the three tall, narrow windows. Outside minute diamond stars lit the fall sky. As Mrs. MacLynn had said, the office was on the side of the manor nearest the stables. A neatly manicured lawn stretched gently toward the moonlit, low-roofed buildings bordered by white fencing. She watched as a light breeze rolled dry leaves toward the corral. They skittered and danced gracefully until the wind abandoned them to fall in the dust of the training paddock.

"Listen, I'm sorry about trespassing. I know I shouldn't have left the road or tried to bluff my way out once I was caught," she said.

Behind her there was silence.

Charlie continued to stare out the window, although her sight was turned inward, reviewing her own behavior. "He's

46

a beautiful animal, Mark. I don't blame you for keeping close watch on him. That spot in your case will definitely be filled next May. If the speed he displayed in the meadow is any indication, he'll lead the Derby field all the way to the finish and the roses."

Still he was silent.

She had groveled, apologized, complimented him and yet there was no response. Exasperated at his quiescence, she reeled. "What do I have to say, Mark? I'm sorry this afternoon ever happened."

He was leaning against the trophy case, his arms folded across his chest as he surveyed her. He still wore the handsome tweed jacket but had loosened a number of shirt buttons. Her gaze was drawn to his chest. Midnight-furred and sun-bronzed, it stirred her imagination. She recalled its hardness, and the stirring beat of his heart under her hand as he had crushed her to him earlier.

Mark was unaware of the effect his display had on her. He studied her attractive silhouette, the way the brown wool clung to her softly rounded, firm breasts and flat stomach, the way it led his eyes to the alluring curve of her hips and long, graceful legs.

"I'm not sorry it happened," he said. "In fact, I rather enjoyed it."

Charlie stepped away from the window. His massive desk sat in the center of the room, separating them. The soft lamplight highlighted the thrust of her breasts as she leaned forward on the desk top to confront him. "Look," she pursued. "Let's just forget the whole thing. I made a fool of myself. It was very unprofessional. I am only here to do a job."

"Ah, I see what's got your dander up." He slowly unfolded his arms and moved toward her. "You think your professional integrity is in jeopardy because I kissed you."

Her red curls tossed as she denied the charge. "No, that's

not it. I placed myself in a situation I had no right to be in."
She didn't care for the gleam in his coal-black eyes as he
approached the desk. She stood upright, striving for a stal-
wart front. "Is that all you wanted to see me about? If so, I
do have an awful lot to do to prepare . . ."

Mark smiled. The deep lines near his finely sculptured lips
gave him a rakish look. "Not at all," he said. "I only wanted
to know how we could help you and Jack get the story you
want."

It wasn't the response she had expected. Flustered, she
brought her hands together and shrugged. "Well, I'd like to
give you details, but until I actually have some visible evi-
dence, about all I can do is collect data from the staff and
family."

He towered over her now, and she found herself short of
breath. "I will admit my research was sketchy in regards to
the spirits, which makes the presence of a psychic
researcher a necessity. A call to the station should produce
someone. I hope that another ghost hunter won't upset your
schedule."

"Not at all," he murmured. "However, I might suggest you
confine your investigation to the ghosts and leave the horses
to their trainers."

Her face was shadowed and turned away from him. Her
magnificent auburn curls lay on her soft flushed cheek,
tempting him to brush them aside, tilt her perfect, ivory
chin up, and gaze into the intoxicating depths of her eyes.

"I wasn't thinking this afternoon when I discovered that
magnificent colt, Mark. Would you believe me if I promised
not to wander off again?" Charlie said. "My mind was on
other things, not ghost hunting."

She felt his hand brush softly against her hair and looked
up to find an amused gleam in his eyes.

"I'm not opposed to a discussion of our . . . er, run-in earlier," Mark said lightly. "Or a refresher." He confiscated one

48

of her slender hands and raised it to his lips, one eyebrow raised questioningly.

Charlie pulled away. "Please, Mark. It was a mistake. I've apologized. Can't we forget it?" she pleaded. His touch was torture; it whet her appetite for forbidden fruit. She had chosen to close the door firmly on all physical relationships long ago. Her reasons were still valid, despite the way this man managed to decimate logic with his nearness. She was far too aware of his luxuriant wealth of raven locks, of the hard, squared set of his jaw. She remembered the sinewy strength of his arms as they had encircled her that afternoon.

He loomed before her, the breadth of his shoulders almost blocking out the lamplight. His face was in shadow, yet there was no mistaking the smoldering look in his eyes. Charlie felt her grasp on the conversation slipping. It would be so easy to lose herself in his embrace, to experience the exhilaration of his kiss again.

"Forget it?" he said. Before she realized his intention, Mark had pulled her into his arms. "Can you forget this?" His lips were gently insistent, probing. She twisted in his arms, afraid the insane wildfire would reclaim her and banish reason once more. Her resistance was faint as his lips crushed hers. Charlie felt herself losing the battle.

She was pliant, yielding. His touch thrilled her, fostered a yearning deep within her that she had forgotten existed. Of their own accord her arms encircled him, her lips opened, and her questing tongue met his eagerly.

Charlie's surrender inspired Mark, staggered him with her response. Her lush, lithe body was pressed to his, malleable to his will. He wanted to bury himself in this ardent enchantress and make her forget his churlish behavior that afternoon. She gasped as his hand slid beneath her sweater to her breast and pushed aside her lace camisole to fondle the silky mound, to brush the rosette tip. He tore himself from her lips to trace the exquisite symmetry of her features, to taste the perfection of her tilted eyes and the velvet of her cheek.

Charlie marveled anew at the feelings he aroused in her. She loved the feel of his muscular arms crushing her and the inferno that his kiss brought to life. It blazed with an intensity that threatened to consume her. Mark's lips were feather light on her brow, his breath warm as his teeth played with her ear. Her own touch was timid as she traced his wide shoulders and the sinewy muscles of his back through the silky texture of his shirt.

"Oh, Charlie." His soft burr caressed her name. A thrill ran through her, sending delicious chills along her spine. His lips found hers once more and plundered their sweetness. "Trespass where you will," he murmured. "I could never deny you."

She was drowning in his touch, his kiss. But the one word penetrated her consciousness. *Trespass.* She had trespassed earlier on forbidden property. Now it was in his world. She didn't belong. She had forbidden herself the chance to be hurt again as Phil had hurt her. She was tasting forbidden delights, forgetting the pain, forgetting the devastation. Trespassing.

Charlie came to the surface fighting for breath, free of her turbulent emotions.

Mark was aware only of her withdrawal, of the renewed struggle as she broke free of his encircling arms. He could feel the feathery touch of her hair as she shook her head in denial against the hardness of his chest.

Anger surged through her. Whether it was a rejection of Mark or of her own reawakening sensuality, Charlie was not sure. In a reversal, she suddenly clung to him, burying her face against his chest, her own arms once more wrapped securely around his waist. "No," she whispered in a tortured voice. "I can't."

Mark didn't hear the pain in her voice. He focused only on

the wording of her cry. "Can't!" His hands were cruel as they bit into her shoulders. There were tears on her cheeks when he stared down into her face. "What do you think I'm asking, Charlie? You haven't taken a step back in time—even in this household. It's the twentieth century, lairds don't seduce house guests anymore."

She flinched at the harshness in his voice. It bit into her frayed nerves, shattering the sensuous spell he'd woven so deftly.

She moved away from him. "I have principles," she said, venting her anger on her sweater, tugging it down into place. "I'm on assignment for one thing. And for another . . ."

His contained fury was a wintery blast. "Isn't one enough?" he asked scathingly. "So you don't mix pleasure with business. I don't give a damn about your ideals. I didn't intend to go quite this far, but you were a very eager participant. Professional ethics can go to hell, Charlie. I want you. I thought you wanted me."

She did want him, painfully so, she admitted to herself. "Mark, I . . ."

His eyes scorched her with their touch, stripped her. "It's not your body that is unwilling, Miss Arden," he said. His tanned, lean finger traced a circle around her breast. The hardened nipple thrust boldly upward through her sweater, refuting any statement she could make to the contrary.

Charlie tore herself away from his grasp. "At least I know I met the real Mark MacCrimmon today," she spat. Icy blue fire flashed in her eyes. "At the paddock."

Passion blazed as he surveyed her, his expression arrogant. He leaned back, perching with ease on the desk top, one gray flannel clad leg swinging loosely. He removed a package of menthol cigarettes from the top drawer and tapped one out. "And which witch did I meet out there?" he demanded. "Make up your mind, Charlie. I've run into two sides of your coin. One hot, one cold."

"I don't have to ask which you prefer," she snapped. "I don't want to be here any more than you want me to be. But I have a job to do, and I can't let anyone get in the way of it."

A smirk was frozen on his chiseled features. "I've had your job thrown in my face quite enough. So often that I'm hard-pressed to believe it is your reason for refusing."

Charlie's chin came up defensively. A martial look lit her blue eyes. "It isn't any of your business one way or another."

"Isn't it?"

"Okay," she conceded. "I'm at fault as well, but that doesn't mean you have to push the issue. Can't you just accept my reasons?"

Mark set a cigarette to his lips. It dangled loosely, giving him a tough, no-nonsense appearance. She was reminded of the man he'd been that afternoon. Inflexible. Hard. His voice had the ring of cold steel. "Perhaps I could if I actually knew them."

Charlie felt she couldn't face him, couldn't explain. "It sounds silly," she placated. "But we are from two different worlds. What good would a quick romp in the hay do us? I can't afford to be distracted from the project. A lot hangs on it. Not only for me but for others."

A squat, tortoiseshell lighter flickered before his face, highlighting its rugged planes before they were obscured by a cloud of smoke. The tip of his cigarette glowed like a tiny beacon. "That's a crock, Charlie. What's the real reason?"

Exasperated, she dropped into the armchair before him. "Hell, it is the truth, Mark. But I doubt if you'd believe me even if I talk myself blue in the face." She put a hand to her forehead, wearily shading her eyes. "If it makes things easier, just throw us out. Or me out. There are other reporters who can make something out of the hauntings."

A tendril of smoke wafted toward her. "I'm sure there are, but none quite as distracting as you, sweet. You can't tell me you haven't run up against similar situations."

At that her fist hit the dark leather arm of the chair vehemently. "Yes, I can," she said emphatically. "My life has been free of masculine harassment. I don't have distractions, complications, or involvements. I can't allow them."

"Or won't." His eyes were shrouded in the smoky haze.

Charlie felt they bored into her, seeing her vulnerability where he was concerned. "What difference does it make? It will be impossible to give the story its proper perspective if I let this"—her hand waved toward him and back to her own breast—"thing continue."

Mark tapped the growing length of ash from his cigarette into a large ashtray to his left. "Distractions are best dealt with, Charlie. Not run from. That's what you are doing."

"I don't think so," she said.

"Have you ever considered meeting things head on?"

"I am!"

"No, I mean a real confrontation."

She was puzzled.

Mark drew his cigarette, silently surveying the lovely woman in the chair across from him. The brightness in her eyes and flush on her cheek told him she hadn't managed to crush the memory of the embrace. "Say we hadn't stopped but had continued to enjoy each other, had spent the night making love," he said.

She blushed and lowered her gaze to the clenched hands in her lap. "I'd never be able to complete the assignment here. I couldn't bear it, Mark."

"Why not? I've found it best to be rid of distractions."

"But that's what . . ."

"Running away still leaves the tension, the curiosity, Charlie. Will you be able to forget me so quickly?"

He was too experienced in seduction. Legions of women had probably thrown themselves against that intoxicating broad chest, had felt his arms crush them, molding them to his tall, hard muscular frame. What did she know about

Mark MacCrimmon other than that he devastated her neatly ordered life? No, she wouldn't forget him or the passion that swept reason away when she was in his embrace. The memories would torture her. If she succumbed to his will and made love with him, would she be haunted with a host of her own ghosts? The shades of his caresses had plagued her all evening, increasing the tension when they did meet. Imagine the emotions that would arise from their grave after years of celibacy if she did surrender!

"I'm not convinced that what you suggest would make concentration any less illusive," she said dryly.

He ground the cigarette out. "You'll never know until you try it."

"Perhaps never knowing would be preferable."

Mark shrugged. "I prefer to dispel mysteries rather than create them." His smile was warm, enticing, amused. Challenging. "Sleep on it," he recommended.

Charlie pushed to her feet. "Perhaps I will. It has been an eventful day."

It was a sin for any man to possess such natural grace, she thought as Mark got to his feet and preceded her to the door. She stepped past him into the cool, echoing darkness of the hall, anxious to put distance between them and the temptation to rescind her decision. The physical link she felt with Mark made coherent thinking nearly impossible.

She glanced up at him, overly conscious of the ardor mirrored in the inky depths of his eyes. "Good night, Mark," she said.

His hand on her shoulder prevented retreat. With calculated patience he tilted her chin upward with the tip of his finger. "Good night, Charlie," he answered quietly and bent his lips to hers. The lightness of the kiss seared her, Mark's breath on her cheek as he drew back fanned the embers burning within Charlie's breast. Mark sensed the spark, saw it in her face, and felt it in the softness of her lips. It shattered his rigid control. He reclaimed her ripe mouth.

She responded instantly, clinging to him a long moment before she tore herself away from his grasp, and like Cinderella at the bewitching hour, flew from danger up the wide, shadowed staircase. The fear that tightened her throat was of her own creation. She had almost surrendered, careless of the consequences. The knowledge lent wings to her heels.

"Sleep well, sweetheart." Mark's voice followed her, reverberating in the empty hall, dogging her footsteps. The deep, musical sound of his voice haunted her even on the opposite side of her bedroom door as she leaned breathlessly against the solid oak. *Sleep well*, he'd said. That, she knew, was impossible.

Chapter Four

IF THE CRISP autumn air was especially invigorating the following morning, Charlie Arden was the only resident of MacCrimmon Manor not affected by it. She arrived at the breakfast table to find the room deserted by everyone but the quaint little form of Mrs. MacLynn.

"I hope you don't intend to take one of my coffee cups out the door, Miss Arrrden," the housekeeper said, eying the reporter's slim frame and the dark circles under the young woman's eyes. "You should have a nice, proper breakfast."

Sleep had eluded her. When she had slept at last, Charlie had been disturbed by vague dreams. Once she could have sworn someone stood at the foot of her bed. But when she woke, her door was still bolted from the inside. A silly precaution, still one she'd felt necessary after fleeing Mark's embrace.

Without asking, Mrs. MacLynn began dishing up bacon and eggs from the sideboard.

Charlie accepted the chair the housekeeper indicated, sedately pulling her skirt over her knees in the event Mark put in an appearance. She hoped she looked determined and efficient in her gray suit. She wished she felt that way. "I will admit I rarely have more than coffee or toast, Mrs. MacLynn," she said. "But your bacon smells delicious."

"You need more than a few rashers to keep your strength, Miss Charrrlie. All those news programs of yours must have you burning the candle at both ends! I'm surprised you have any meat on you at all."

Charlie smiled but only played with the nutritious breakfast the housekeeper placed before her. "I hope I didn't oversleep and upset your schedule, Mrs. MacLynn. Am I the last one down?"

The little woman grinned. "Ah, they're all off at cock's crow, miss. The laird is training the colt. Mr. Don went off to a breakfast meeting somewhere, dragging Miss Gwen with him. Your Mr. Donahue was anxious to develop his film and went off to the television station. And that Miss Rinehart"—the housekeeper dismissed the medium with a careless wave of her hand—"she's never up till half the day's done."

Charlie forced herself to eat. She nodded to the adjacent chair, inviting company. Mrs. MacLynn settled herself, her plump arms folded cozily on the table. "Do you suppose Mr. Donahue got some nice photographs of the ghosties, miss?"

"I hope so," Charlie said. "Have you seen any of them, Mrs. MacLynn? The ghosts, I mean?"

"Of course I have," the woman said. She smiled, her expression dreamy. "The manor's my home, Miss Arrrden. I was just a wee thing when my parents left the Highlands with Mrs. James. Angus and I were bairns together." She sighed. "It's hard to believe Angus is gone. He was so full of life."

"So you grew up at MacCrimmon?" Charlie sipped her coffee slowly. It was rich, delicious. After all the paper-cupped, convenience-store coffee she'd grabbed en route to the station, the delicate, painted china teacup was pure luxury.

Mrs. MacLynn nodded. "My Brian was one of the grooms, as was my father. My mother was a maid."

"It seems you're part of the family," Charlie commented.

"Of the clan, aye, miss. The laird minds his own."

"Angus MacCrimmon?"

Mrs. MacLynn nodded. "And his son Mark. The new laird has a heart of gold. After what those others did to him, it's surprising he still has such a sweet temperament," the housekeeper said.

Charlie wondered if they were speaking of the same man. But her curiosity was piqued. "What others, Mrs. MacLynn? Members of the family? The ghosts?"

The housekeeper wasn't to be drawn though. "Ach, I've been babblin' again. Excuse me, miss, but I'll just get back to my kitchen, if you're finished?"

"Oh, yes, certainly," Charlie said. "If you could spare me a few minutes when Jack returns, I'd like to interview you about any ghostly occurrences you've experienced." The woman beamed. "Is there a phone I could use to contact the station?"

The housekeeper's gray head bobbed. "The laird said you were to use his office, miss. I'm to assure you he'll not be needin' it today at all."

Charlie stared into her coffee long after Mrs. MacLynn had gone about her duties. The offer of his office was very generous on the surface. Did Mark have ulterior motives though? Could she remain impassive, able to make coherent decisions about the program, or would she be tormented working in the room that had been the scene of their showdown? It would be impossible to push thoughts of him away, she decided. Yet, until Jack returned with the results of his time-lapse pictures, she couldn't very well plan the next step of the ghost hunt. She had to focus on the living instead.

The statement the housekeeper had made concerning Mark reminded her how little she knew about any of the MacCrimmons. Katrine Rinehart bore looking into as well.

It was shocking to realize how ill prepared she had been for this assignment. She would have to remedy the omission immediately. Since the lion had offered his den, she was foolish not to make use of it. Charlie finished the last of her coffee and marched out of the room.

Becky, the research assistant at the station, was eager to shelve all other projects to dig for Charlie. She promised to call later in the day with something. *Anything*, Charlie requested. She was desperate to give a direction to her interviews.

When she dropped the receiver back on the cradle, Charlie was once more at loose ends. She sat in the large, comfortable chair behind Mark's desk and tried to make notes. Instead she found her fingers trailing along the highly polished dark grain of the desk top, touching the squat lighter, the crystal ashtray, the dark leather of the chair arm. Her thoughts refused to stay on the filming ahead. They strayed to the conversation of the night before.

Could he be right? If she acceded to his wishes and went to bed with him, would he be out of her system? It had been so long since she had been so attracted to a man, she doubted the answer was that simple. Perhaps for him, but for her?

Avoiding him was impossible. It was his home. In fact, it was his ancestors that she was supposed to be investigating. More confrontations were bound to occur. Would she retain enough self-control to deny Mark? Or was she being a ridiculous prude?

Jack's arrival did nothing to relieve her mind.

"Got some great shots," he said, dropping into the chair she had occupied the previous evening. "Not all were of the ghosts though."

Charlie frowned at him. "What do you mean? You did get something we can use? A hoax already?"

"Nope." He grinned. "See for yourself." Three photographs sailed toward her. "I blew these up for you rather than include them on the proof sheet, Chuck."

She straightened the pictures out. The angle of Jack's lens had been wide, encompassing a large section of the entrance hall and massive staircase. The time of each shot was displayed digitally in the top left hand corner of each photograph. She was amazed to find the camera had picked up vivid details despite the dark. She wasn't as pleased with the subject matter.

Each photograph was of her. One showed her descending the staircase in an almost stealthy manner. The time was a few minutes after midnight. On the next picture she was looking up into their host's handsome face, her expression dreamy. The light from the open office door bathed them in radiance. Time: 1:30 A.M. In the last she was clinging to him shamelessly, responding to that final kiss. 1:35 A.M.

Jack watched as her face paled, then flushed beet red. "There were some shots that might be your ghostly visitors," he said, diplomatically changing the subject. "Look at these." He tossed her a sheet of proofs, columns of miniature photographs all neatly numbered in his precise hand.

Charlie tore the incriminating photos of herself into small pieces and dropped them in the ashtray. "Which ones in particular, Jack?" She picked up the larger sheet.

"Seventeen through twenty-five. Here, this might help." He passed her a magnifying glass. "See the faint light or glow to the left of the staircase?"

She nodded. The image looked like the reflection given off by the crystal of her watch when the sun struck it. But there had been no sun when the clock registered 2:20 A.M.

"It moves up the staircase and fades in a succession of pictures," Jack pointed out. "My second camera kicked in at two A.M. The first didn't register anything of interest . . . ghostly interest, that is."

"Forget about the other shots." She got up and went to the

doorway, looking out into the massive hall. "Just where were your cameras set up?"

Jack led the way to a shadowy corner. "Right over here, Sherlock. What's on that suspicious mind of yours?"

Charlie stared thoughtfully at the double set of tripods he had left standing, then at the high, narrow slits of the windows. "Could moonlight shining through one of those windows cause a reflection on the lens of your first camera but not touch the second?"

"Mmm. Maybe, but I doubt it. They were both set to catch a wide angle of the room. Besides, the other exposures don't give a hint of light. You can see the difference when the light goes out in the office on the proofs from the first roll of film." He refrained from mentioning the subject matter of those particular photographs. "If I have my directions right, you wouldn't get any light, sun or moon, shining directly for a reflection," he added.

Charlie stared up at the medieval embrasure. "Why? It may not be much because of the depth of the casement, but it wouldn't take much either."

"Not when the windows face north."

"Damn. Well, so much for natural causes. Besides me, who else did you tell you were putting your ghost trap into effect?"

"No one. Did *you* know where I had them set up?" he asked, beginning to dismantle the first tripod.

Charlie gave him a look of pained amusement.

It cheered Jack considerably.

"Don't be ridiculous." She gave a quick, searching glance around the room. "Could someone come up with the same effect with a flashlight? I don't necessarily mean using the camera lens, either. Anything. Any bit of glass, something shiny to reflect an indistinct form like the one in the picture."

Jack relaxed. This was the Charlie Arden with whom he

was used to working. She had the ball and was running with it. "We could try to duplicate it tonight," he suggested.

"Great," she said and stalked off to investigate different angles to perpetrate her hoax. It kept her partner from seeing the listless expression in her eyes. All her enthusiasm had been forced for his benefit. Just because she hadn't noticed the camera setup didn't mean one of the others hadn't. Mark in particular. He had been out of the room when she arrived. Although that had been at midnight and the pictures hadn't been taken until almost 2:30, he could have found the tripods and returned later to create the ghostly images. The man had the uncanny ability to move noiselessly, and he would know every inch of his home. Perhaps there were secret passages to consider. The manor was old enough. What was Mark's motive, though? At dinner he did not seem particularly interested in his brother's political career.

"We ought to try our hand at duplicating the spirit photos early though. I'd hate to disrupt a regularly scheduled ghostly appearance tonight," she said as Jack completed the demolition of his last tripod.

"Mmm. Why wait for dark when we could steal away to the dungeon," he said casually.

"A dungeon! Not even this mausoleum could have that, Jack. It might have when it was in Scotland, but Laird James' widow, Jane Steele MacCrimmon, doesn't sound like the type of woman to move a dungeon even if she did transplant the manor."

"Basement then," he conceded. "I'd have to see it first, but chances are it's windowless, dark, and dank. What better hunting ground for a haunt?" He gathered a tangle of aluminum tubing together and rattled it for effect. "Let me put my chains away, Sherlock, and I'll meet you in the culinary charmer's den."

Charlie smiled. "The kitchen?"

"The kitchen." He dashed up the stairs.

Tim Tierney leaned on the fencing and stared across the dirt track. An exercise boy was walking the chestnut stallion after a strenuous run. "He looks real good," Tierney told Mark, who stood at his side. "Outgrown the skittishness and lengthened his stride nicely. Endurance over the distance is increasing, too. Angus would be real proud of Pride if he could see him."

"Yeah, Dad is beside himself with joy," Mark MacCrimmon said, lowering his field glasses. He tipped his head in the direction of the horse and rider as they pranced around a bend in the track. "Named him right, didn't we, Tim? Angus's Pride."

Tierney grinned, bringing lines to the ruddy complexion beneath his bristling, full beard. "Your dad was a good judge of horse flesh. Bred this colt himself, at least on paper, I understand."

"That's right. And Pride'll father his share of winners, as well," Mark commented absently. "Pop's banking on it."

The older man had the eerie feeling that Angus Mac-Crimmon, although dead over two years now, had communicated with his eldest son recently about the young stallion.

Angus's Pride danced, eager to get the bit between his teeth and run. His small head tossed. His dark mane flared out. Jimmy, the young exercise boy, grinned proudly from the stallion's back, keeping his mount to the cooling walk Tierney had ordered.

"I'd like to put a jockey up. I think it's past time. Jimmy handles him well, but he isn't the man I want up at the post."

Mark nodded and stepped out on the track to meet the equestrian pair. "Any suggestions?"

"Jaffee?"

"Okay. Get him."

"You're sure?"

The laird stopped and waited for Pride to reach him. The colt pushed his nose toward Mark's jacket pockets. The ever-present lump of sugar was awarded absentmindedly as the laird stroked Pride's soft, damp muzzle. "I thought you wanted Jaffee," he said.

"Well, I thought maybe you'd want someone else."

Mark gave the trainer a lopsided grin. "Like Francie?"

Tierney felt the need to expiate himself, to explain. "She's got good hands."

"Let's try Jaffee," Mark said. "When can we get him out here?"

"Day after tomorrow." Tierney's eyes sparkled in the sunlight. "I anticipated a bit. Gave him a call. He's interested but won't commit. He wants a winner pretty bad."

Mark patted Pride's muscled chest. "We've got one." Pride whinnied in agreement, and the men laughed.

"He's got a high opinion of himself, sir," Jimmy said fondly of his mount. "And he wants to run. I had a hard time holding him back today."

"Patience, Jim. You'll get to ride the hurricane yet," Mark said. "Give him a good rubdown and some oats."

The boy nodded and turned the chestnut toward the stable.

Mark and Tierney watched them go.

"I'm thinking of letting him out tomorrow, Mark. See just what he can do," the trainer said.

The laird started. "Mmm? Sorry, Tim, my mind was somewhere else."

Tierney repeated his suggestion and added, "We've never actually timed Pride yet."

"Sure, go ahead. Whatever you think is best." Mark's tone was abstracted.

Tierney hoped he hadn't blundered by bringing Francine Voight's name up.

"Mind if I use your office, Tim? I lent mine out and have a phone call to make," Mark said.

"Be my guest." The old trainer doubted if his employer actually heard his answer. He was already on his way to the tack room.

It didn't take long for the call to go through the Duke University operator. It did take a few minutes to locate Bill Wynstand.

Mark hadn't seen Wynstand in five years. Bill was busy teaching. And his passion for sailing kept Wynstand coastbound year round. Time fell away when Mark heard his old roommate's voice. Wynstand hadn't changed much over the years. He still had one Achilles' heel that MacCrimmon was willing to tickle.

"Mark! Don't tell me you've finally decided to let me loose among those artifacts you call furniture!" All through their college days Wynstand, a history major, had tried to interest the MacCrimmons in donating the ancient furnishings of the manor's entrance hall to a museum. Naturally, Wynstand had pictured himself as curator then. Each holiday he'd been frustrated to find the MacCrimmon clan bound for tropical islands to escape the cold, snowy Midwestern winters. Wynstand had always hoped they would celebrate lavishly at the manor by inviting a well-deserving young historian to fondle the heirlooms transplanted with their ancestral home.

"I need a favor, Bill."

Wynstand crowed. "Ha! Finally I have you where I want you, MacCrimmon. I can't guarantee anything without at least a week's invitation."

Mark chuckled. "With or without Lois?"

"Without naturally. Give a guy a break, Mark. The woman hounds me day and night." Wynstand sounded anything but henpecked. He sounded proud. "'Sides, she's visiting her sister in Florida. She just had twins and needed Lois's expertise."

"How are the brats?" Mark asked of Wynstand's own set of identical boys.

"Great. Seventh grade now and away at school," Wynstand said. "I'll be there tomorrow. Now, what's this favor?"

Mark told him.

Wynstand gave a low whistle of astonishment.

"I know it's short notice, Bill, so just do your best. Not too much trouble, is it?"

"Hey, buddy. Are you kidding me? I wouldn't miss this for the world."

Charlie Arden and Jack Donahue emerged from the dark stairwell looking more like chimney sweeps than reporters.

"Did it have to be a coal bin?" Charlie asked with a pained expression as she caught sight of the black streaks on her sweater.

"Women," Jack moaned. "I thought you wanted dark conditions for these phoney ghost shots."

"I did, but . . ."

"Looking for a darkroom?" a deep voice asked.

Charlie could have sworn Mark hadn't been there a moment before. Just the sight of him lounging in the open doorway started a warm glow in the pit of her stomach.

Mark thought she looked adorable with the coal-dust smear across her nose.

Charlie flushed, nervous. What was the matter with her? She was a moth flittering close to his flame, singeing her wings badly in the process. The whole situation was not just combustible, it was volcanic. How could she possibly continue with this assignment? She was a guest in his home, dependent on his whims. Maybe if things had been different, if they'd met under other circumstances . . .

Jack took his cue from Charlie's bright cheeks. "Nope. Ghost hunting."

His partner looked at him aghast. "Duplicating an effect to verify authenticity," Charlie clarified. She fervently hoped that the pictures came out better than the disappointing reflection they'd managed to manufacture.

Mark nodded sagely. "Any luck?"

"Some," she said.

"None." Jack encountered a seething look from his associate. "Some," he echoed. "Maybe."

Their host's eyes twinkled with amusement. "I have some news for you. That parapsychologist you wished for will arrive tomorrow."

Charlie's face lit with interest. "Gwen came through then. Great."

"That's not all," Mark warned. "Kat is determined to honor us with a séance tonight."

"Determined?"

Mark shrugged. "I tried to dissuade her."

"I'll bet you did," Charlie muttered.

His grin widened. She sounded jealous.

"A bit sudden, isn't it?" Jack asked.

"Kat is consumed with the idea."

Charlie sighed. All she wanted was a long hot bath and an early bed. A faint pounding at her temple threatened to mature into a bonafide migraine. She put a hand to her forehead, unconsciously leaving a new smudge. "I'm sure she is. We can be ready, can't we?" She glanced at Jack.

"Cinch," he said.

"Okay. Where and when is it to take place?"

Katrine Rinehart sat in solitary splendor in the large armchair, her low-cut, black, sequin-covered bodice twinkling in the flickering candlelight, her eyes closed, her hands loosely clasped in her lap. She appeared to be unaware of the activity around her. Charlie doubted the sincerity of the woman's pose. Katrine favored the theatrical far too much to convert the reporter. Choosing the ancient hall as the setting for the séance appeared logical since the majority of the apparitions had manifested, according to the witnesses, in the oldest section of the manor. Insisting on the bewitching hour, however, had been Kat's own contribution.

The medium hadn't been content with location and timing. She was determined to set the stage as well.

Mrs. MacLynn bustled around the hall followed by two amused stable hands, drafted for their brawn. On Kat's orders all electrical current to the hall had been shut off. Now the only illumination came from the ancient wall sconces and candelabrum. The hall danced with shadows.

Kat's only concession to the twentieth century was the TV camera. The Channel 5 team recognized the gleam in the medium's eye. Kat was star-struck.

To complete the macabre setting, a massive, round oak table had been moved to the center of the cold floor and surrounded with four hard-backed chairs. Kat herself had requisitioned a comfortable wing-back armchair and set it to face the staircase.

Mark leaned against the doorjamb of his darkened office, watching the proceedings. A cigarette dangled from his lips, the glowing tip a firefly compared to the candlelight. The somber colors of his sports coat, shirt, and tie blended into the gloom. He watched the preparations with a resigned lack of interest.

Charlie admired his cool, and wished she could emulate him. Her stomach was twisted in knots of anticipation.

"Ready, Chuck." Jack patted the minicam on his shoulder. The station call letters were emblazoned on its side. "Any specifics?"

Her red curls tossed. "Wing it. Just don't miss anything."

He laughed at the plea.

Mrs. MacLynn finished lighting the last candle in the large chandelier and nodded in Gwen Hale's direction. Shadows flitted across the housekeeper's face as the flames danced in the ever-present draft. Jack set his film in motion, recording the artistic yet ghastly temporary disfigurement of the woman's features. He tilted back to follow the ancient fixture, which rose as the stable hands hauled on a thick rope pulley. The chandelier swung gently, a glittering pendulum over the table. Jack refocused on Charlie's pensive face as she stared up at it. When she noticed him she grimaced and made a slashing movement across her throat to halt the film.

"I think we're ready," Gwen declared, gliding over to the table. Her heels barely echoed on the stone floor. "Kat?"

The medium slowly opened her eyes. Her face was serene, her smile confident. "Yes," she breathed.

The other participants seated themselves, eager to get the séance over and past. Kat nodded placidly, indicating that Mark and Don should take the chairs on either side of her. Gwen took the chair next to Don's, leaving Charlie no choice but to accept the seat Mark held for her to his right.

Kat's arms stretched toward each of the men, her long scarlet nails turning her hands into claws. "Please join hands so that we have an unbroken circle," she whispered.

A chill that had nothing to do with the proceedings ran through Charlie when Mark's hand clasped her own. His face was solemn, registering concern for her. She knew her looks were not at their best. She felt haggard, tired, and vulnerable. The circles under her eyes were more pronounced in the candlelight. The warmth of his large hand covering hers was comforting. She felt protected, and yet the chill remained. Perhaps she shouldn't have worn the lavender dress. The silk fabric was thin, though the dress was high-necked and long-sleeved. It clung to her tall, slim figure. She remembered the flare of desire she had read in Mark's eyes at her entrance, the way she had felt consumed by his gaze. Wishing she could let her guard drop, Charlie reached for Gwen's hand. Business came first.

She had gone straight to her room for a quick shower and clean clothes after learning of the séance. The afternoon had consisted of interviewing the housekeeper and members of the household staff who claimed to have seen apparitions. The interviews had been inconclusive. Charlie wondered if she'd use any of the clips in the final product. With luck, the séance would yield something of value for her story.

"How's the sound level, Jack? Are you picking everyone up?" Her eyes checked the tiny microphones clipped to each person at the table.

Jack barely glanced at the recording gear. "Yeah, fine." The sensitive device picked up the sound of his voice. The needles swung right, then dipped left once more.

Kat took deep breaths. On a fleshier woman the exercise would have been erotic. Kat looked pathetic. "I will be going into a trance shortly," she said quietly. Don't be frightened. I am perfectly all right. No matter what happens, remain seated, keep the circle unbroken.

"My control is a young French girl named Linette. She died during childbirth in 1924."

Once again Kat closed her eyes, tilting her head back slightly. She swayed. The only sound in the room was that of the medium breathing. Charlie realized she was holding her breath. Did the other participants feel this tense? She glanced at Mark and wished she hadn't. He winked in reassurance and squeezed her hand.

He was striking in the soft candlelight. The blue-black color of his hair shone. She longed to run her fingers through its soft, inky waves.

Becky, the researcher at the television station, had called late, just before Charlie had gone down to dinner. The information she relayed had been disturbing. It made Charlie view the handsome laird with different eyes.

Kat's breathing became ragged, drawing Charlie's attention away from her host. Kat groaned.

"It shouldn't be long now," Gwen whispered. "She's almost in a trance."

Charlie looked at the blonde suspiciously. "You're sure?"

Gwen nodded. "I've attended a number of séances. My mother has been trying to contact my brother for years."

Kat groaned again, more loudly this time, then her head dropped to her chest.

"She's in a deep sleep," Gwen said. "Linette should be along shortly."

As if she's the neighborhood Avon lady, Charlie thought.

They sat in silence. From the corner of her eye, Charlie saw Jack move to the other side of the table, his camera never leaving the medium.

Charlie's eyes traveled to the limp figure of Kat Rinehart. Was the woman a con artist? Unfortunately, Charlie knew little about her subject matter and the people concerned. Her gaze moved around the table. Next to the medium, Don sat very still, his expression one of extreme interest as he watched the entranced woman. Was he waiting for a signal from her, or was he the one calling the shots? If there was a mastermind running this ghostly scam, Don MacCrimmon was an excellent candidate for the position. His gaze shifted from Kat to Gwen and he smiled confidently at her. A signal? Charlie stared at the table where Don's hand covered Gwen's. His hands were well-manicured, soft. The only truly masculine feature was the light scattering of dark hair along the back. They weren't hands that labored physically, like his older brother Mark's.

Don's coat sleeve was pushed back slightly from his wrist so that his watch was exposed. The dancing flames from the swinging chandelier were reflected by the watch crystal, creating a mesmerizing sight. They reminded Charlie of a Beardsley print of fairy creatures of gracefully swaying fire creatures, or perhaps ethereal nymphs from the spirit world. It was a fanciful thought, but so was the idea that she was sitting in a drafty Scottish manor waiting for a message from the dead.

Kat raised her head and looked at the group seated around her. Her gaze lingered over the darkly attractive men, then measured the women. "*Bon jour*," she said. The tone was deeper, richer than Kat's normal speaking voice. She held herself differently, more assured. The low-cut dress no longer looked pathetic; it was sophisticated.

Don leaned forward in his seat. "Linette?"

"*Oui, monsieur?*"

"Thank you for joining us this evening."

Kat's thin shoulders shrugged in a graceful Gallic movement. "It is nothing. Katrine makes all possible."

"Is there anyone who wishes to speak to us this evening?"

Linette's laugh was light and fanciful. "I think *you* do not wish to speak to *them*."

"Are there any that once lived in this house, Linette?" Gwen asked.

The medium's head cocked slightly to one side, as if she were listening to someone behind her chair. Silence.

"Linette?"

"*Non*," came the answer.

"No?"

"*Non*. No one."

Gwen and Don exchanged a puzzled look. But then stared across the table at Mark.

"Don't look at me," he said. "I didn't do anything."

"You've always been more attuned to them," Don insisted.

"Ask after someone, Mark," Gwen urged.

"They aren't here," he insisted. "This is your party. Ask yourself."

Charlie sighed. "Linette?" she asked.

"*Oui, madame?*"

"Last night, was there a visitation?"

Silence. Charlie persevered. "Do you know if there was a visitation?"

"*Oui.*"

"Who was it?"

"Him."

"A name, Linette? Do you know his name?"

"He will not give it."

Gwen jumped at the answer. "He's there with you?"

"*Non,* he has gone."

"Damn," Don murmured under his breath. "Linette. Could you describe him?"

"He is gone."

"Did he leave a message, Linette?" Gwen demanded.

"*Non.*"

"Will he return?"

"*Oui.*"

"When will he return?"

"He will return."

Gwen sighed. "We aren't getting anywhere with this."

"Linette." Mark felt Charlie flinch as if his voice had startled her. He squeezed her hand, comforting her. "Since no one wishes to communicate tonight, I think you can restore Katrine to us."

"If that is your wish, *monsieur.*" She sounded disappointed with his request.

"It is, Linette."

Silence again fell on the group. They watched as the medium's head rested once more on her chest, then her eyes fluttered, and she awoke. Eagerly, Kat looked at the faces around her.

"What happened to everybody?" Don demanded. He pushed his chair back, the legs scraping across the stone.

"After all these weeks, they pick this night to absent

themselves," Gwen said, disgusted. "Why?"

Self-conscious, Charlie wiggled her hand free from Mark's firm grasp. "Maybe they're camera shy."

"There were no messages?" Kat blinked, disbelieving.

"Not a one," Jack told her, hefting the camera from his shoulder. "Maybe there was a convention they had to attend."

"Linette came through?" Kat insisted.

"Oh, yes," Gwen assured her, putting an arm around the woman's shoulders. "It wasn't your fault, or hers."

"Well, I could use a drink," Don announced. "Anyone else?"

Charlie nodded. She felt chilled to the bone.

"I wonder who the mysterious man was that Linette mentioned," Gwen said.

Mark held the door as everyone filed into the warm lounge, drifting toward the bar. "It was Dad."

"Dad!" Don exclaimed.

"Angus?" Gwen's forehead wrinkled in thought. "What was he doing here? Why didn't he contact us?"

Jack eased himself onto a stool and leaned back on the padded edge of the bar. "More importantly, how do you know?" he demanded.

Mark removed a bottle of bourbon from the mirrored shelves and began pouring shots into tumblers. "Nothing special, I just feel him. I recognize that it's him."

"And do you see him?" the cameraman pursued.

Mark grinned. "I think everyone has thought they've seen him in the last two years." He handed Charlie a tumbler. "Drink up. It will make you feel better."

Her hands were ice cold. "Thank you."

Don added an extra measure of bourbon to his own glass. "It isn't like Dad to show up without a reason," he insisted.

"He'll be back." Mark grinned. "Linette said so, didn't she?"

Jack sighed. "I suppose I'd better set up the cameras again." He downed his own drink quickly.

Mark was still at her side, Charlie realized. "Are you all right?" he inquired. Concern was mirrored in his eyes.

"Of course. Just tired, I guess. It's been a busy day." She sipped at her drink.

"All of it," he urged.

"I should help Jack," she said.

But her partner waved Charlie off when she joined him in the hall, Mark still at her side. "Get some sleep, Chuck," he advised and patted the twin cameras. "Hansel and Gretel don't need babysitting."

"You're sure?"

"Go to bed!" He already had the tripods erected. "Get her out of here, would you, Mark? The woman's dead on her feet and too stubborn to admit it."

"But I'm not. Or I wasn't," she said. "It's the funniest thing, but I feel really drained since the séance." She forced a laugh as she moved to the stairs. "You'd think I'd been the one giving a performance instead of Kat."

Mark dropped an arm lightly around her shoulders and led her up the stairs. His strength warmed her, chasing away the chill that even the whiskey hadn't cured. She was vulnerable. She wished she could huddle in his embrace, feel the hard length of his body pressed intimately to hers. Sanity ruled her days, but now in the dim corridor she hungered for more than the iron-clad promises she'd made to herself.

They reached her door all too soon, and the comfortable, secure cocoon of Mark's presence began to unravel. "It's a busy day tomorrow," he said, taking her hands in his own. He was surprised at their icy feel. They were so small and fragile in his larger hands. "You *are* cold, sweetheart."

She flinched at the endearment, the same term he'd used to abuse her at the paddock. If only she could go back, change what had happened.

Mark pushed the door of her room open and guided her to the sofa near the cold hearth. He settled her against the soft cushions and pulled a comforter from the bed to tuck around her before kneeling at the fireplace. In no time he had a fire blazing.

"Better?" he inquired. "Feeling warmer?"

Her almond-shaped eyes peered at him from the huddle of blankets as she nodded.

She was so defenseless, he thought. She didn't know what had happened. What would probably keep happening, despite his own attempts to stop it. He didn't know why *they* were so interested in Charlie. Was it Charlie herself or his attraction to her that had redirected the attention of the spirits?

Mark ran a hand wearily through his hair. "I think there's something you should know," he said, sitting down next to her. He pulled the tie loose at his collar and unbuttoned the top button of his shirt.

Her rosebud mouth emerged from the comforter parted in surprise. Becky's call was very fresh in her mind. Was he actually going to tell her about Farley?

Her glistening red lips tempted Mark sorely. He wanted to take her in his arms as he had the night before, to kiss her into submission, to evoke the passion that so enchanted him. Instead, he took her blanket-wrapped form in his arms, cuddling her close under the pretense of warming her.

"About the ghosts," he began.

"Ghosts?" Charlie swallowed her disappointment. "What about them?" she asked.

The laughter she had often seen in his eyes was absent. He was serious, she realized. "I think they are using you."

"I don't understand," she said. "I don't believe in them. How could something that doesn't exist affect me?" She grinned at him, eager to find a joke in his words.

"That doesn't mean anything, Charlie. How did you sleep last night?"

She frowned. "All right, considering."

"Any dreams?" he asked.

Charlie turned her head to stare into the fire. "Fleeting ones."

Mark watched her averted profile. "What about?"

Her lips twisted wryly as she glanced back at him. "Persistent, aren't you. Who's the reporter here anyway?" Her annoyance faded when she saw the worried look in his eyes. "Okay, okay. I think they were pretty typical really, Mark. Vague. I even thought someone was watching me once."

"And?"

"And nothing. It's a dark, brooding mansion you have here. I just had a gothic dream."

"But the séance made you cold?"

"Mark, it's October. The hall is drafty, and I was ill-advised enough to wear a light dress. Don't read something into my foolishness."

"Charlie, you don't understand," he insisted. "They exist only through human agencies. Us. The cold, your dream . . ."

He was serious but she could not be. "Hush." she shrugged an arm free to lay a finger against his lips. "I know you mean well, but there aren't any ghosts. You're doing a wonderful sell job. I'm just not buying. Thank you for the fire. I'm quite toasty, so you've more than fulfilled any expectations a guest could have of her host."

Mark wished he could forget he was host to the news team. His arms tightened around her. If she refused to listen, he would have to watch after her himself. Not that it was a chore. More like a delight, one he realized he would relish twenty-four hours a day.

"All right. I tried." His eyes softened and he smiled down into her upturned face. The soft lavender silk of her dress clung provocatively to her breast where the comforter fell away from her shoulders.

"Would you like to see Pride work out in the morning?" he asked.

"Pride?"

Mark grinned. "Your protégé. His name is Angus's Pride."

"The chestnut colt?" She smiled up at his shadowed face. "I'd love to."

"I'll have Mrs. M call you then. You won't get much beauty sleep. We work him just after dawn."

"Only a few hours away." If he asked her to share them with him, what would she answer? Last night her response had been almost violent. She'd done a lot of thinking since then. No, brooding. But she hadn't come up with an answer.

"Charlie?" His slight brogue touched her name. She loved the sound of it.

"Yes?"

Dear God, Mark thought. How could he leave her? It felt so good to have her nestled in his arms, her lips so close, so sweet, so tempting. It was agonizing to release her, to stand up. "I'd better leave so you can rest. Sleep well."

She nodded. "Good night, Mark. Thank you for the fire."

His hand dismissed her appreciation casually. "Good night, Charlie."

He was actually leaving, she realized. Charlie stood, the comforter dropping away forgotten, and took two steps after him. "Mark!" Her fingers closed on his sleeve, gripping the muscled arm beneath. "Mark, wait."

He turned, puzzled by the urgent tone of her voice, pleased to remain, even for a short while.

Charlie restrained an impulse to throw herself in his arms. "Mark, I'm sorry we had such a bad beginning. I wish it could be erased. But we can't go back or start over."

His fingertips caressed her cheek, turning her face

upward. "No, we can't, Charlie. We could continue with a better understanding though."

She nodded fervently. "Move slower," she agreed. Or had she meant to suggest it?

"Not too slow," he said. "We had a hell of a start."

An impish grin lit her pixy face. "We did, didn't we."

In answer, he gathered her possessively against his chest. Their lips met and clung.

Charlie was shaken by the depths of her feelings for this man. She barely knew him, and yet she was beginning to realize her life would be quite empty without him.

Their embrace lacked the voracity of previous ones, yet the wildfire coursed through her veins. When they parted, she relished the desire mirrored in his eyes. Mark held her closer, brushing her burnished curls back from her face. "It's very hard to leave you, Charlie Arden. Very hard." He tasted her lips once more, then put her aside firmly. "Sleep well, little love."

Her eyes were stars, he thought. A universe he longed to explore. Still, a new beginning had been made. A much more advantageous one.

"Good night," Charlie whispered.

With a supreme effort of will Mark reached for her door and closed it, shutting her in the bedroom alone. Charlie leaned contentedly against the wood, listening to his footsteps recede down the hall. He was whistling. The sound echoed cheerfully in the corridor.

Yes, tomorrow was going to be a very special day.

Chapter Five

DESPITE ONLY A few hours of sleep, Charlie woke before dawn, eager to greet the new day. Her spirits were buoyed with anticipation at spending time with Mark. Her eyes gleamed softly in remembrance of the tenderness he'd displayed, the concern in his vibrant baritone, the way her pulse increased its tempo at his touch. Charlie hugged her pillow, wishing momentarily it was the hard, lean body of her handsome host. He would be excitingly insistent, she knew, dominating her softness, inciting the passions and feelings she had suppressed for so long.

She bolted from the bed, embarrassed at the turn her thoughts had taken. She blamed the early morning chill of the room for the erect nipples pushing at the silk of her gown. Although she considered rebuilding the fire in the fireplace, she had no time to linger here. She pulled the filmy negligee over her head and wiggled into brushed-denim jeans, cable-knit pullover, and boots. The comb pulled at her tangle of red curls as she hastily tidied her hair and applied a light coat of mascara. There was no need for blusher; her cheeks bloomed.

Mrs. MacLynn was surprised when her timid knock was answered immediately.

"Don't you ever sleep, Mrs. M?" Charlie asked, unconsciously using the family's pet name for the housekeeper.

Mrs. MacLynn noticed and grinned warmly at the young woman. "I could ask you the same, Miss Charrrlie," she said. "He's waiting for you on the terrace. The door in the dining room opens on it directly. If you'd like some coffee . . ."

But Charlie was already past her, pulling on a jacket as she flew down the stairs.

Mark looked just as he had that first afternoon at the paddock. Could it possibly have been only two days ago? Charlie paused at the glassed terrace door, amazed that this man could make her blood race even when he was unaware of her presence.

Mark stood gazing out over the formal flower beds, his breath a cloud of vapor in the cool dawn air. The blooms of all but bordering chrysanthemums had long since gone to seed and had been removed by a gardening service. But Mark seemed unaware of the stark symmetry of the landscape as he waited impatiently. She could sense the restrained energy, see it in the set of his broad shoulders beneath the weather-beaten leather jacket. Faded Levi's molded tightly to his muscular thighs and flared slightly over low-heeled boots. Cowboy boots. He had a penchant for the West, she realized. His working clothes were just that, made for hard work around the stable, for long hours in the saddle. Fleetingly, Charlie thought of the sketchy biography Becky had given her on Mark MacCrimmon over the phone. Her spirits sank as she recalled one very valid reason for Mark's partiality for the West. Then he turned as if he sensed her presence, a welcoming smile in his eyes, and her morning righted itself. The disturbing past, his and hers, was shelved, forgotten for the present. She wanted only to bask in the intoxicating gaze of the master of MacCrimmon.

Charlie was out the door, her feet flying, to meet the outstretched hands of her lover. It didn't matter that their intimacy had progressed no further than stolen kisses. The hunger was there. She read it in his face, and she knew he recognized it in hers. They were lovers.

"Ready?" he asked.

"Oh, yes."

His startlingly white teeth flashed against his deeply tanned face. "Is it the reporter or the girl who is so eager?" he teased, black eyes dancing.

"I haven't been a girl for a long time." She grinned. "But the reporter doesn't start work until after breakfast."

Mark dropped one of her slim white hands and pulled her toward a path that wound away from the house. "I may never let you eat again, woman," he said. "Pride started his workout half an hour ago, but Tim has orders not to let him out until we get there. Afterward, I thought you might like a tour of the farm." He glanced sideways at her. "An official one, guided by the laird, if you'll have him."

Charlie responded to the laughter in his voice. "I'd love it," she said. "I've always wanted to find out what goes on before a horse actually comes to the starting gate."

"Professionally?" Mark asked, hurrying her through the brisk fall morning air. Above, the sky was beginning to brighten to a soft blue-gray, as if it were sluggish on waking and undecided on whether the day would be clear or cloudy.

She matched his long stride effortlessly. "Worried? No need to be. I'm just a horse enthusiast."

"Just how much do you already know, Charlie? I don't want to feel like a fool explaining elementary things."

"Well," she said slowly, teasing, "I can ride and I can handicap races. Everything in between is virgin territory."

"Handicapping!" His brows rose in surprise. "How did you ever get interested in that?"

She reveled in his astonishment. "I practically grew up at Churchill Downs," she informed him smugly.

Mark snapped his fingers. "Hal Arden."

"My dad."

"All right, Miss Arden." He grinned. "Now that I know you for a ringer, I'll definitely watch my step." He halted at the corner of the stable and waved his arm in a theatrical, courtly bow that would have done his noble ancestors proud. "Voilà, our humble track."

Charlie peeked around the stable to find a small but efficient race track. A beaten oval of earth enclosed a grassy infield, separated by white fencing and marked at intervals by taller posts painted bright red. The chestnut colt she'd admired at the paddock stood impatiently on the soft brown earth. He was saddled and had a slim rider. The small, lightweight racing saddle appeared to barely cover his broad back sufficiently for the boy who balanced, knees drawn up, in the short stirrups. Both rider and colt seemed enthused at MacCrimmon's arrival.

Mark led Charlie to a place at the rail away from the group of men who waited, the collars of their heavy coats turned up against the cold. One man moved over to join the laird and his guest.

"Good morning," Mark greeted him. "Charlie, you know Tim Tierney, our trainer. And that's Jimmy Newcomb atop Pride. Jimmy, Miss Arden."

Tim and the exercise boy greeted Charlie with smiles and, in Tierney's case, a handshake. They both acted as if outsiders watched the stable's most promising colts work out every morning. Charlie knew that the opposite applied, that they guarded the MacCrimmon thoroughbreds jealously. It was a tribute to their boss that they accepted the presence of a reporter this morning.

Angus's Pride pushed his blowing muzzle toward Mark's jacket pocket. "How's he doing?" MacCrimmon asked, stroking the colt. "Ready to run?"

"You bet he is," Jimmy said, eager to have the wind in his face.

Tierney's bearded face considered the question, his eyes

going over every inch of the chestnut's hide. "Yeah, Mark, he's doing fine. Let's try three furlongs."

Mark linked Charlie's arm cozily with his own and leaned on the fence. "No, farther."

The trainer frowned. "It's the first time we're letting him out, Mark."

"How about at least five furlongs, Tim? And don't let him get the bit between his teeth, Jimmy, or you'll end up with a runaway." Mark turned to Tierney for agreement.

The older man nodded to the exercise boy.

The boy turned the prancing colt back toward the center rail and a point where they'd begin the short race against the clock. Each of the men checked stopwatches in their hands. Mark winked at Charlie. He liked the way her eyes glittered with excitement. They danced and twinkled, seducing him with hints of untouched passion. There was a mystery about her that intrigued him. She was so alive and yet held her emotions bridled with an iron grip at odds with her soft, feminine appearance.

"Go!" Tierney yelled, his shout blasting a vapor cloud in the air.

Angus's Pride recognized that this morning was different. As Jimmy dropped his hands and drove his heels into the powerful shoulders, Pride gathered his strong haunches and jumped forward for the gallop down the ribbon of track. His skin rippled, his small sculptured head stretched out. His thundering hooves echoed back to the breathless group gathered at track side.

The white rail was a blur to the exercise boy, but he recognized the quarter pole as his mount flashed by it. He was up, riding almost on the colt's neck, his weight over the smoothly moving, muscled shoulders. The wind in his face was cold and brought tears to his eyes. It whipped the tiny jockey cap from his head. The half-mile post was rushing at them. He pulled back on the reins, fighting the colt for control a fraction of a second before the well-trained horse recognized the rider's touch and slowed his headlong dash.

Simultaneously, the stopwatches of trainer and watching stablemen locked on a hundredth of a second. Mark held his pocket model so that Charlie could see the time. "My God, Mark, he's . . ."

He gave a small, almost imperceptible shake of his head and turned to the other men. Jimmy and Pride were cantering back around the track, both obviously still eager to run.

Tierney ran his fingers through his beard in thoughtful contemplation. "He isn't up against a field, of course," the trainer said slowly. "We don't know how he'll react to other horses, whether he'll want to race."

A slow smile started at the corners of Mark's eyes and spread to his lips. "Oh, he'll run, Tim," he said softly.

"I'm not saying the colt doesn't have heart, Mark. Some can't stand to see another horse in front of them. Get skittish. Jimmy and Pride have a rapport, too."

Mark finished for the man. "But Jimmy isn't a jockey . . . yet."

Tierney laughed. "Okay, okay. Pride surprised me. I'll admit it. I knew he'd be good, but this!" He glanced at his stopwatch once more before stuffing it back in his pocket. "Let's see what he does with a regular jockey up tomorrow."

Mark's long fingers entwined with Charlie's. She felt a warm glow flow through her body at his touch. Her cheeks were bright, her eyes luminous with repressed excitement when she met his anxious gaze.

"Well, Miss Handicapper, what is your opinion?"

"No contest, Mark. Five furlongs in 55.7 seconds! My money's on Pride," she blurted, her eyes going once more to the sleek young stallion as Jimmy brought his mount prancing up to them.

The boy's face was flushed, exhilarated. "How'd he do, sir?" he asked, cautious, almost afraid to hear the results.

Mark let go of Charlie's hand as Pride pushed his nose across the fence, eager to claim praise. MacCrimmon grabbed the bridle straps and gently pushed the questing muzzle from his jacket pocket, all the while stroking the soft line of the colt's forehead. "You both did extremely well, Jim. In fact, I don't see why you can't start wearing the silks this spring in some minor races. Providing you don't grow anymore."

Jimmy's face brightened considerably at his employer's words. "Yahoo!" he yelled. Pride whinnied his own excitement and tossed his head as if the verdict concerned his future as well. "Oh, thank you, sir. Thank you. I'll do my best. Promise. And I won't grow!" the exercise boy pledged.

The men exchanged amused looks before Tierney brought them back to reality. "Don't keep that colt standing, Newcomb. Cool him down!"

Jimmy saluted merrily and turned Pride back to the track, carefully holding him to a walk.

As the others went back to their duties, Charlie continued to stare after the boy and colt, now on the far side of the field. Mark leaned back against the fencing, content to watch the play of thoughts across her face. The soft curve of her cheek tempted his gaze to follow the graceful line of her throat, on to the exquisite shell of her ear barely visible beneath a riot of sunset curls.

"Mark." Her husky voice interrupted his concentration. "Why hasn't Pride raced yet? It seems unusual for a two-year-old, especially one like Pride."

"Because, my adorable newshound, he's a little young for his age," he said, still intent on her profile.

Charlie turned, surprising a look of fascination on his rugged features that was instantly wiped away in a teasing grin as he captured her hand once more. He turned her away from the track toward the stable.

"As you no doubt know," he continued, lecturing now,

"all thoroughbreds have an official birthday of January first. It doesn't matter when they are born that year. We date their birth as New Year's Day. Naturally, the dames don't all foal then. We try to breed them for spring foalings. Pride was an exception. More of a mistake really."

"A beautiful mistake," she corrected him, twisting to watch the colt once more.

Mark sighed. "If only I could claim as much attention as he does," he said.

Charlie grinned at his dramatics. "How did it happen?" she asked, ignoring his forlorn expression. "The mistake, that is."

"It was the mysterious case of the eager jumper," Mark intoned. He adopted a stilted English accent reminiscent of old cinematic murder mysteries. "I remember it like it was yesterday, my dear Miss Arden. The sting of winter was in the air, promising an early snowfall. The animals' coats were quite shaggy, a sure sign of a long, hard winter to come."

She knew he was enjoying himself by the way the laugh lines deepened at the corners of his dark eyes. "Very picturesque," she said, playing along. "Pray, do continue."

"Picture this, my dear," he continued. One arm snaked around her shoulders. The other arm gestured with a sweeping movement, as though he were drawing a curtain aside. "The pretty little mare alone in her corner of the field, nibbling daintily on the crisp, brown blades of grass. The breeze rustling the barren branches above her turns, carrying her delightful scent to the eager swain. Unbeknownst to our heroine, naturally."

"Naturally," Charlie agreed. She enjoyed the feel of his arm resting casually on her shoulders. Mark's lips swept near hers as he bent toward her. The scent of his aftershave was heady. Her lips parted. "Then what happened?" she asked.

"The inevitable." Her breath against his cheek defied the tight control Mark fought to preserve. His eyes dropped fleetingly to her ripe mouth, then he straightened, leaning back against the white fencing once more. "Lachlan scaled Morna MacDonald's white tower. Or in this case, his own and her fencing."

"Lachlan? You mean his sire is Lachlan Sawyer?"

Charlie whistled softly. "No wonder he's got speed. Lachlan brought home purses of over two million in his career."

"Three and a half million," Mark said. "But who's counting? It wasn't record earnings. But he earned his leisure as a stud. Morna was a promising filly until she hurt her knee. That ended her racing career and began her breeding one."

"I don't see how the result of such a romantic story could be a mistake."

Mark's mouth turned up on one side in a half-smile. "Only in the timing, sweetheart. The match had been made on paper. We just hadn't foreseen Morna going into heat when the stallion was in the next field. Mares go into heat every twenty-one days, but we prefer to have spring matings. Gestation is eleven months, so foaling comes just before the supervised matings. Pride unfortunately was foaled the third of October."

Charlie smiled and leaned back against the fence, her arms folded across her chest, content to listen to her host all day if necessary.

"I guess not everyone agrees that a man's fancy turns to love in the spring," she said.

"Lachlan certainly doesn't." Mark's eyes softened as he looked down into her face. "Nor do I," he added.

Charlie wasn't ready to let the conversation turn personal yet. She was nervous, unsure. She pushed away from the fence, away from Mark, and took a few steps to look out over the fields, past the stable. "Didn't you promise me a tour?"

He was immediately ready to comply. "Yes, I did. This

way, enchantress, to choose your courser."

Inside the stable the large gray gelding stood nibbling idly on a bit of straw. He hadn't been saddled yet but wore a vividly colored saddle pad. Mark stopped to stroke the damp muzzle and murmur to his mount before guiding Charlie toward three sleek horses a little farther down the aisle of stalls.

Charlie chose a stately strawberry roan mare over a smaller brown mare or chestnut gelding. Mark approved her choice with the comment, "Brietta shares your coloring. You'll look well together."

She could have said the same of him astride Madoc, his gray.

Mark saddled both horses himself, easily swinging the heavy western saddle from the side of the stall to Madoc's back. A smaller, highly decorated saddle was hefted to Brietta's back over a Mexican-weave blanket. Although she hadn't been riding in years, Charlie swung effortlessly into the saddle.

Brietta's lope was smooth, tireless, as they followed the gray down a bridle path of packed earth between meadows. Charlie adapted to the gait, standing in her stirrups, reins held loosely to allow the roan freedom without relinquishing control.

The landscape they traveled was breathtaking. They passed gently rolling fields and glens of wild, tangled wilderness resplendent in green, gold, orange, rust and yellow hues. Bird songs filled the air. Squirrels chattered at their intrusion, then scampered away into the heavy undergrowth. And everywhere they went there were horses: beautiful, sleek, long-limbed horses in every conceivable color. Many a blowing nose was thrust over the fence in recognition of the laird, or in pursuit of the seemingly endless supply of sugar cubes in Mark's jacket pockets.

His knowledge of the estate was intimate. When they dismounted in a wood, he moved through the underbrush silently. Charlie followed, careful to step where he did, hardly daring to breathe. Their stealth was rewarded by the sight of a sleeping fox, of a majestic owl who eyed them solemnly before deciding they weren't worth his consideration, of a matched pair of wild rabbits nibbling on a bit of scrub brush. Charlie was amazed at the apparent lack of fear displayed by the animals. Either they accepted the dark-haired man as one of their own, or he was an excellent woodsman who knew how to keep upwind of the creatures. Her own presence caused no uproar, perhaps because the animals accepted her as Mark's mate.

Charlie blushed at the fanciful idea, thankful that Mark's gaze was turned away at the moment. She dwelt on the thought though. So much about the man fascinated her: his quick sometimes quirky smile; the way laughter danced in his eyes; the way his thick black hair grew in waves, curling along his collar. His muscles rippled beneath his tautly stretched shirt as he swept a low branch out of her way. She inhaled the manly smell of him combined with that of leather, horses, and the autumn foliage.

Two days ago she had considered the MacCrimmon family snobbish jet-setters. The man who sat at ease in his saddle near her, a cigarette dangling loosely from his lips, his low-crowned Stetson tilted over his eyes, was none of these things. Yet, according to Becky's research, he was president of MacCrimmon Enterprises, a breeding and racing concern. He owned property in Louisville, was on the board of a bank. His employees affectionately called him the laird. The title rode easily on his broad shoulders as if it didn't bring responsibilities with it. And she knew instinctively that Mark carried the burden unselfishly. He was lord of this realm, but he was proud of its natural beauty, not of the fact that he possessed it.

"You really aren't what I expected, you know," she said.

Mark tossed his cigarette in the dirt beneath the horses' hooves. "Am I not, sweet Charlie?" he asked, his burr turning her name musical. "In what way?"

Brietta responded to the light touch of Charlie's heel and moved next to Madoc on the roadway. "I don't know how to put this delicately."

Mark's white teeth flashed in a wolfish smile. With an intuition that scared her, he asked, "A snob?"

"Yes. No. Oh, don't make it so hard. You know what I mean."

His gloved hand clasped hers on the reins. "Yeah. You're wondering why I'm different from Don, right? He fits the mold. I don't."

Flustered, afraid she'd unwittingly insulted the family, Charlie stuttered. "I . . . I don't mean to say Don, or Gwen for that matter, are . . ."

Mark's easy laugh halted her apology. "Compared to me, they are snobs. You see, Charlie, there are two different trains of thought in this family. There's Imogene's whirlwind social club, and Grandmother's simple goals.

"Dad and I subscribe to the uncomplicated life that my Grandmother, Jane Steele, loved. She wasn't interested in hobnobbing with the rich and famous, but when her father, my great-grandfather, decided to launder his reputation and millions with a European title, Jane was a dutiful daughter. She married Laird James MacCrimmon and adapted to the clan life immediately, although her husband made no effort to smooth the way for her. He had married a bank account, not a bride. He did give her a child, my dad, then dashed off to be a hero in the first world war. Grandmother once told me she started packing for home the day she received word that James had been killed. She brought the manor over brick by brick. The breeding farm was started by her with MacCrimmon stock from the Highlands."

Charlie patted her mount's sleek neck. "She sounds like a

very interesting lady. I wish I could have met her," she said softly.

"She'd have liked you."

Charlie glanced up at the affection in his voice.

Mark shrugged. "Anyway, the other members of the clan followed the money over. Imogene, Gwen's mother, represents the society-conscious side of the family. Although they are two generations removed from the clan, they still use MacCrimmon in their name as if it were a badge. Imogene herself courted any old family with money. She married well and still flits from one upper-class party to another. When we were growing up, Gwen and Don spent more time with her during the holidays. I had this consuming hobby." He gestured toward the estate. The expression in his eyes was dreamy as he looked across the verdant fields and patches of forest. "I wouldn't give this up for any of their affairs. The land gets in your blood. Especially the bluegrass. There were things that fascinated me about the West. I tasted it all, the deserts, the mountains, the plains. Then I came home."

He laughed shortly. "Sorry. I didn't mean to ramble on."

"Don't be sorry." Charlie's curls danced as she shook her head. "It's a beautiful tribute, Mark."

He had shaken the mood off though. "Come on. We have one more spot to hit. A highlight of the tour, Miss Arden. Not everyone gets this included for their entrance fee."

The sun was cresting above as they entered a small clearing surrounded by evergreens. In the center sat a neat little cabin, a small stable, and a fenced paddock.

Mark halted the gelding at the edge of the wood and leaned forward on his saddle horn, a quirk to his brow as he looked at her. "What do you think?"

"Oh, Mark," Charlie breathed, awed. "It's beautiful."

Truly beautiful, she thought. Not predisposing like the manor, the cabin was built almost entirely of rough, quarried stone. It was a single story high with a steeply sloping roof and wide chimney. A hitching rail rose from a blanket of late-blooming wildflowers before the door.

Charlie turned eagerly to her host. "Whose is it? Can we go in?"

A boyish grin lit his face at her response. "It's mine, of course."

The interior of the cabin was just as charming as the exterior. Basically one large room, it was compact. A small kitchen and bath were separated from the living area by half-walls. The large fireplace dominated the room. A piece of Pueblo pottery and two intricately woven baskets decorated the massive mantlepiece above it. Vividly colored Indian rugs covered a polished wooden-plank floor. A large, U-shaped, *Yei*-figured rug hung above a narrow, antique, double-poster bed. Another textile, with a procession of figures worked into the weave, was thrown casually over the back of a long sofa before the fireplace.

It was cold inside the cabin. Although clean, it had a vacant feel. It seemed to be waiting. Charlie shivered, then smiled at her own fancy. She missed the heat of the sun.

"Make yourself at home," Mark suggested, draping his own discarded jacket over her shoulders. "I'll start a fire."

Charlie hugged the coat nearer. "I could use some coffee."

"In the kitchen," he said, busy igniting a pile of tinder.

When she returned to the main room, Mark was placing a log on the now raging fire. "Relax and warm up," he suggested, taking the coffee cup she handed him and sipping it. "I'll go see to the horses. Back in a few minutes."

Charlie smiled uneasily at him. The close quarters inside the cabin made her shy in his presence. "You seem to always be building fires for me," she said.

"I'd like to do much more," he told her, then playfully touched the end of her nose. "Now, take advantage of the heat."

She sank into the soft cushions of the couch, hearing the

door close behind him. The jangle of bridles and the soft thud of hooves followed his voice as Mark praised the animals. The sounds receded until only the snap of the flames remained.

How pleasant to escape to a sanctuary like this one, she thought. The cabin wove a cocoon of comfort. The stone walls barricaded one against the pressures of the outside world. Here there were no news cameras, no ghosts to hunt. The atmosphere of the place didn't allow for their existence. It was the kind of place she'd once dreamt of as a girl, an ivy-covered cottage.

Charlie slid to the floor and stared into the fire, her knees drawn up, her back against the sofa, her coffee mug balanced between her hands.

When was the last time she'd felt so content to let time pass her by? There had once been a period in her life when deadlines were unheard of, when she hadn't cared if she had a career, or a way to make in the world.

Once she had been naïve and trusting. Once she had been in love, or believed herself to be. Phil had made her feel so alive in his arms during those forgotten times. Forgotten feelings.

How unsuspecting of Phil's real character she'd been. *Unreasonable*, he'd called her when she'd taken an instant dislike to the friends he brought home. *Close-minded, narrow, straight*. God, how he had laughed at her arguments! But she'd remained true through it all. Even the women. She had worked to support him through college, then continued to work when he insisted he needed his own print shop. Couldn't work for the fools who ran the other shops, he'd said. They limited his creativity, shackled his freedom. As she had. He had told her that so often. Phil, the man who had whispered high-sounding promises on moonlit nights to the impressionable teenager she'd been. The man her high school friends envied because he was a man, not a boy. Phil, who strutted, preened in their adoration, and demanded her devotion, giving none in return. Phil, who had tried to teach her how to hate. Not him, but herself. For Phil had hated her.

In the five years since the divorce, she still could not understand why he hated her. Why he blamed her for everything, especially his arrest and conviction for forgery. The creativity he boasted had conjured up the ingenious scheme of printing counterfeit currency. She drove him to it, he had said. That was an excuse, of course. She didn't believe it. She did let it color her judgment though. After trying so hard to create a perfect marriage, to live as she'd thought her parents should have lived, trying to make their life together last, it was difficult to admit her life with Phil Wilson had always been a mistake. And it was a mistake she feared making again.

Mark returned to the cabin and watched his suddenly thoughtful guest. Instinctively he knew that she wrestled with an inner turmoil. He longed to take her in his arms, tell her . . . tell her what? He didn't have the right to buffer her against the world, and she refused to entrust him with the pleasurable task. Charlie wasn't a simple-minded airhead like Farley. She was a successful newswoman. She had a will of her own. He couldn't just breeze into her life and expect her to fall into his arms—or his bed. It wasn't a casual attraction. Had never been. The more he came to know her, the deeper his feelings grew. He wanted her, not just her body, but the inner woman he couldn't touch. Her soul. The intangible thing that made her so desirable, enchanting, infuriating, maddening. What made her Charlie.

Silently Mark pulled off his boots, leaving them near the door from habit. He poured himself a fresh cup of coffee and brought it to the sofa. She didn't seem conscious of his presence when he stretched out full length on the cushions behind her.

Outside the sun blazed down, but within the thick walls

the lighting was dim. The pines near the house shaded the room year round. At times he had considered cutting them away. But today Mark welcomed the dim light, the play of the firelight on the quiet woman.

She was so delectable, so lovely. It was torture to be so near her and have to restrain himself. He'd made the mistake of rushing her before. The memory of her response, the answering ardor, burned brightly in his mind, making concentration on business nearly impossible. He hungered for the molten touch of her lips, the soft, yielding curves of her body crushed in his arms.

Unable to resist, his fingers lifted one of her short curls and watched it coil trustingly around his knuckle. He was glad they were soft curls. Her hair was luxurious and thick. Burnished lights danced, flickered over the short cap, drawing his eyes to the clusters at the creamy nape of her neck.

Charlie turned slowly, twisting to look up into his face as he reclined on the couch. Her blue eyes were deep pools, troubled, afraid.

"Mark." His name was a throaty whisper.

He leaned over, briefly touching her lips in a gentle kiss.

"Mark," she said again. This time it was a plea.

He swung his legs around and slid to the floor beside her, taking her in his arms. Charlie melted into his embrace, returning the breathless kisses he showered on her upturned face.

The sweet smell of spring filled his head as her lilac perfume reached his senses. It was uncomplicated, natural. Yet she was confusing and complex. He tasted the captivating curve of her cheek, the exotic shape of her eyes, the dainty contour of her earlobe, the tender, volatile hollow of her throat.

Charlie trembled, spellbound as he robbed her of reason and sent her spinning into a staggering world of sensation. She had hungered for so long unknowingly. Each touch of

96

his lips sharpened her appetite, increased the insistent, throbbing pulse at the base of her throat, fostered the building glow of desire in her stomach.

Charlie sat back, disentangling herself from Mark's arms. He reached for her but received a steady, resolute gaze from her passion-glazed eyes. They smoldered, as unbanked as the burning timbers in the fireplace. Sapphire flames licked, caressed his face, his chest, his lean, flat stomach, and along his long, muscular legs.

She bent to remove her boots, but his hands were there first, drawing them off. Charlie was silent, content for the moment to see herself reflected in the deepening ebony shadows of his eyes. Her breath caught at the desire reflected there.

And yet Mark waited, watching for a sign from her.

Slowly Charlie peeled her sweater off over her head, tossing her amber-flecked curls.

He gazed in fascination as the woman who had held him at arm's length dropped the sweater at his feet and began loosening the buttons of her blouse.

Her fingers shook, making her fumble with a button. Mark's hands joined hers, slowly pushing the cloth aside, exposing the pale, creamy mounds of her breasts. She was small, but in his eyes no other woman had been as perfect. She was both delicately built and delicately hued. The faint, sun-kissed glow of her shoulders lightened to a milky white near the pink, hardening peaks of her breasts. His gaze caressed her. Her breath was shallow. It quickened when he dropped her blouse to the floor and bent to taste the honey of her mouth once more.

Her lips clung to his, making it difficult to discern which of them was the seduced, which the seducer. She longed to press against him, to revel in the feel of him against her naked flesh. The need to do so frightened her. It had been so long since she'd given herself, even longer since she had wanted to do so. Her knowledge of men was limited to Phil Wilson, and Mark was nothing like her ex-husband.

Tentatively, her hands rose to Mark's broad shoulders. Her fingers brushed gently at his blue-black hair where it curled over his collar. It was silky and thick. She knew its texture and the faint scent of autumn that clung to him. Her exploration continued. Her fingertips moved down his arms, tracing, stroking, discovering the sinewy strength concealed beneath the flannel of his shirt.

Mark kept a tight rein on himself as delicious chills preceded her touch. He heard more than felt the metal snaps open as she pulled on his shirt, her fingers pushing the garment off his shoulders, down his back. He released her briefly to rip it off, then drew her closer, flesh against flesh. She sighed and melted against him, threatening his sanity. In answer, his lips slanted against hers telling her of his need. His hands spanned her waist, her ribs, until his thumbs touched the underside of her breasts. She was like velvet: smooth, warm, and lush. He could feel the flutter of her heart beneath his palms. The staccato beat was an echo of his own, as steady, hard, and swift as hoofs on a race track.

He had enjoyed lazy lovemaking with other women, but this was different. Charlie needed the excruciating, seductive, slow pace. She was awakening like Sleeping Beauty from a self-imposed slumber. Oh, and how lovely she was as she welcomed him.

Charlie met his lips eagerly, tasting and tantalizing him. Her tongue met his, caressed it, stroked it, and invited further entry. Her arms encircled his neck, her fingers buried in his thick jet waves and pulled him down, sliding beneath him on the soft nap of the rug.

Mark supported himself above her, their flesh a breath apart. He stared down into her eyes, losing himself in their passion-darkened depths. She tasted of nectar, and he found it impossible to have enough of her. Yet he was in no hurry it impossible to have enough of her. Yet he was in no hurry to take all she offered. The chase was not over. It wouldn't be until he discovered every private nook, every sheltered valley of her being. He would do so at leisure, savoring every moment.

When his lips moved to the hollow of her throat, Charlie arched toward Mark, her breasts brushing against his chest. Her arms tightened, urging him to crush her closer. She was no longer reluctant, but anxious to consummate her need of him. She wanted him. The throbbing insistence of her own body was new and demanding. And if the hot, rushing madness in her blood had not told her she wanted him, her heart had. She wouldn't be complete until she was one with him. She would never be whole without him. Her hands entangled in his hair, Charlie drew Mark's mouth back to hers, telling him of her urgency with her touch, her lips, her tongue.

"Not yet," he whispered hoarsely against her lips. Catching her questing hands, Mark held them, drawing her arms up to hold them captive over her head. He smiled down at her and, ever so slowly, he lowered his mouth to her breast. When he nipped playfully at one thrusting nipple, Charlie gasped with pleasure. His tongue circled it, teasing.

"Mark," she pleaded. She twisted her hands, trying to release his hold, wanting, needing to touch him in return.

"Patience, love," he said against her skin. His free hand slid along her rib cage, across her quivering stomach, then paused infinitesimally before moving lower, dipping into the waistband of her jeans.

Charlie's breath was a long, drawn-out whisper of pleasure. "Maaaarrrk, I . . ."

His mouth was back, accepting her ardent need. This time when Charlie's hips arched against him, Mark released her wrists.

Her fingers slid up his darkly furred chest to his shoulders,

She was parched, thirsting for the taste of him. It had been so long since she had allowed anyone to touch her. The sensation was more wonderful than she had remembered. Better, for Mark did not merely take what she offered. He gave of himself, luring, teasing, and in doing so, driving her to new heights of pleasure.

Slowly he undressed her, marveling at the play of firelight on her alabaster skin, until she lay naked and quivering beneath his hands. He savored the desire in her eyes, in her touch. She was glorious. And she was his.

Charlie was aggressive in her need of him. She pushed him back ever so slightly so that she could explore his broad, muscled chest. Her hand moved lower, following the trail of dark hair to where the hard, swollen length of him pushed urgently against his jeans. He moved against her, letting her know the extent of her power over him. Tentatively, her fingers pressed harder, reveling in the feel of him. She enjoyed the sound of his sharply sucked-in breath as she loosened each button of his jeans.

Her touch was light, soft as a feather, yet irresistible. Mark lost the battle. His hard-won control snapped. His body clamored for the release only she could give him. With a moan, he reclaimed her lips, his mouth demanding and aggressive.

Charlie gasped. Her breathing was uneven and ragged as she gave herself up to the ecstasy of being desired. Her breath was his breath. The beat of her heart matched his, loud and fast.

Mark held her a prisoner of sensation with his lips, playing them from her mouth to the thrusting tips of her golden-hued breasts. And while he held her in thrall, his hands ran down her body, memorizing every soft curve.

Her fingers dug into the straining muscles of his back. "I want you," she whispered hoarsely. Then in wonder, she ran her hand along his jawline. She had only met him a few her hand along his jawline. She had only met him a few short days ago, but the depth of her need surpassed anything she had known before. "I want you so much."

Mark caught her hand and pressed an ardent kiss to the palm. "Come with me then." He leaned back and pulled her up, sweeping her into his arms to carry her the short distance to the bed.

Charlie wrapped her arms around his neck. "This is a fantasy. I dreamed but never thought I would feel this way."

Tenderly, he set her on the bed. He caressed her cheek and stared down into her glowing face. "Dreams come true, love. Mine certainly are." He tossed his jeans aside.

"Let me improve them," she said. She reached up to brush his tumbled hair from his brow, then pulled him down.

He went willingly, lying next to her, his lips reclaiming hers, allowing her to know him and the strength of his passion.

Charlie was beguiled by his response to her touch, but she was soon caught up in even more enthralling sensations as Mark skillfully demonstrated his need of her. His actions lifted her to higher planes of ecstasy. The extent of his patience and passion inspired Charlie. The look in his eyes seared her. And in responding, she inflamed him.

Like a flower, she opened herself to him. She was a sorceress stripping him of his will. She demanded that he claim her in her kiss, in her caress, in the insistent love reflected in the bottomless blue seas of her eyes.

Charlie woke to find herself nestled against a man's broad chest. A muscled arm lay across her breasts, warming her, casually claiming possession of her slim white form. She could feel his breath tickle the back of her neck as they lay curved against each other's body in the bed.

She recalled the delicious sensations he had reawakened for her, first on the rug before the blazing fire, and then again and savored, the sensation of being sated but loath to part from him.

The fire had gone out, but the room retained its warmth. Or was it just the inner glow she had felt since capitulating to Mark's embrace?

She had expected to feel guilty, not ecstatic. It had been so long since she'd felt like a woman. And she did feel that—beautiful, desirable, wonderful.

She wiggled closer to Mark, her hands tracing the hard length of his body. There were a few gray hairs among his dark waves, she noticed. The fact endeared him to her the more.

Mark molded her closer. Awake at her first stirring, he had been content to feel her soft, curved form next to his so intimately. Now he reclaimed her lips, feasting on the tender welcome as she responded. His kiss stirred her to passion once more as he probed the sweet recesses of her mouth. His hands slid from her trim waist up over her rib cage to the warm fullness of her breasts.

Charlie moaned against his lips and pressed closer to him.

Mark was in no hurry. His tongue teased her, moving down her throat to taste the rosy delights of her breasts.

Why had she renounced these delicious tremors, Charlie wondered dreamily? They filled her whole being. Her fingers entwined in his hair. No, she hadn't forsaken passion. She had never experienced such total fulfillment with a man before. Never with Phil. He'd always taken. She'd given. But Mark . . .

Charlie sighed his name. Her voice was ardent, husky. It branded him.

She arched against his hand as it slid up her thigh. Her eyes were sapphire gems, sparkling as she stared into his eyes, unknowingly committing herself to him entirely.

He read the intensity of her emotion. The fear had receded, if only temporarily. What caused the fear? He receded, if only temporarily. What caused the fear? He wanted to know . . . but not now. Now she was his, soft, passionate, yielding, flushed with the glow of love.

Charlie felt her world whirl dizzily, her universe tilt, until the only stable part of the spinning system was Mark. He was here, constant and strong, in the stormy vortex. Sure of her actions, she claimed him, lifting her body to his.

He claimed her, ravenous for her. He was a demon bent on driving the golden Circe beneath him toward a searing peak. She was an angel, a sorceress, a vixen, matching his silent demands, insistent on inciting him to higher planes of pleasure.

In her mind, the carefully constructed ivory tower crumbled as his hoarse voice murmured her name.

Outside the cabin, night began to claim its due, chasing the warming sun across the western sky. The lovers were insensible of passing time. Unable to relinquish the spell, they dressed slowly, touching each other in wonder, fearing the enchantment's dissolution. Mark lingered over the buttons of Charlie's blouse, loath to cover her blushing, pale, silk skin. She stood on tiptoe, arms around his neck, planting little kisses on his beard-darkened chin, memorizing every angle of his face with her lips, cherishing the rough texture of his face as it scraped her cheek.

Dusk gathered, recalling them from the magic of the afternoon. Regretfully, they parted. He resaddled the horses. She banked the fire, destroying the last embers, returning the cabin to its slumber. After a lingering kiss, he lifted her on to Brietta's saddle and swung aboard Madoc's back.

"Darlin' Charlie." The soft burr as he caressed the endearment sent chills down her spine. He leaned from his saddle to kiss her again.

A warm glow ran through her veins. The sudden tightness in her throat brought tears to her eyes. She had taken his advice, had given in to temptation. Had she ever thought making love with him would cure her of the fascination? That it would make it easier to concentrate on her assignment? It hadn't. She wanted more of him. Wanted more from him. It would be so easy to love him. But he would never feel the same about her. Their backgrounds were so different. No, Charlie decided. When it came to wishing for a future with Mark MacCrimmon, she didn't have the ghost of a chance for the dream to come true.

Chapter Six

A STRANGER WITH sun-bleached hair greeted the returning couple. "Fine host you are," he grumbled to Mark.

Charlie looked at the newcomer with surprise as Mark closed the front door behind her. The stranger was almost as tall as Mark, seemed about the same age, but had a distinct middle-aged spread that the blue-gray vest of his three-piece suit did little to conceal. His complexion was ruddy. His eyes were a bright impish blue under bushy, almost white brows.

"Wyn!" Mark shouted with pleasure. "I see you made yourself at home." He nodded to the brandy snifter in the man's left hand.

"Not all MacCrimmons are an uncouth lot," Bill Wynstand remarked, eying his friend's disheveled appearance. "I see the years haven't changed you, buddy boy."

"Can't say the same for you, pal," Mark declared and faked a punch at the blond man's waistline.

Wynstand looked pained. "Must you remind me?"

Mark turned, drawing Charlie forward, his arm draped possessively over her shoulders. "Charlie, meet Bill Wynstand, professor of history. Wyn, Charlie Arden, our resident news sleuth for North American Broadcasting. She's here to catch our ghosts."

They made a handsome couple, Wynstand thought. The young woman's red curls were tossed from the wind. Or perhaps a sojourn in bed. The soft smile in her eyes as she glanced up at MacCrimmon's tall form hinted at the latter. His friend's stance was that of a man guarding something very precious. Mark hovered near her, as if challenging anyone else to try to pry the prize from his possession.

Charlie grinned and thrust a hand forward, all business. "How do you do, Dr. Wynstand? What brings you to Mac-Crimmon?"

"Mark," he answered, taking her hand. "I'm not nearly as stuffy as he makes me sound, Miss Arden. I am enchanted to discover beauty and brains in such an attractively compact package. I thought all the treasures at MacCrimmon were dusty heirlooms."

Charlie smiled. "You'll make me blush, Dr. Wynstand," she said.

"By the way," Wynstand said, "fellow named Donahue has been wondering where you'd vanished."

Charlie looked conscience-stricken. "Oh dear. He's been working while I took an unscheduled holiday. If you'll excuse me, gentlemen, I have just enough time to repair the damage before dinner."

"The spell is broken, and the princess turns into a reporter again," Mark said wryly.

Charlie understood the regret underlying his flippant comment. She slid from beneath his restraining arm with a tender smile. "She never stopped being a reporter," she said and turned to the blond man. "I hope we'll get a chance to talk later, Dr. Wynstand."

"Bill," he insisted. "I'll drink to your eyes."

"Like hell you will," Mark grumbled as Charlie disappeared up the stairs.

Wynstand's eyebrows rose sharply at his friend. MacCrimmon was jealous! After all these years, Mark had fallen in love again. "Well, it's about time, buddy," Wynstand said with approval.

Jack Donahue made himself at home on the sofa in Charlie's room, deaf to hints that she was late and had to get dressed. He had arrived at her door just as she'd gotten out of the shower. Guilty about her afternoon away from the story, Charlie relinquished the room, retreating to the bathroom to complete her toilette.

"Any new developments since last night?" she asked loudly, hoping her voice reached her partner in the outer room.

"I'd guess so," he replied and paused theatrically. "Oh, you mean with our ghosts?"

Charlie sighed, her breath fogging the mirror. "Don't be cute with me, Jack."

"Me?" he quipped in mock innocence. "Set the date yet?"

Frustrated, Charlie stuck her head around the bathroom door. "Jack, be serious."

She looked adorable. Her red curls had become tangled in her haste to dress for dinner, and her cheeks glowed with embarrassment over his broad hints about her afternoon with MacCrimmon.

"I am serious," he insisted. "I'm happy for you."

"You're in left field," she said, ducking back into the bathroom.

Jack wasn't deceived by her protests. "It's about time," he said. "You should have stopped mourning Phil Wilson years ago. Welcome back to the world of the living, Chuck."

"Don't be ridiculous," she recommended. "Now, what did you get last night?"

Jack's tone sobered. "A few surprising specters. And a little more blackmail material."

Buttoning the tight sleeves of her emerald silk dress, Charlie emerged from the bathroom. The mandarin collar was snug at her throat, leaving the simply cut fabric to shimmer over her soft curves. "Let's see," she said, joining him on the sofa.

He handed her the first sheet of proofs. "Look at this." His finger tapped a number of pictures in quick succession. "Quite different from the reflection ones. I'd swear I had a double exposure if I didn't know better."

The photograph showed a faint, fully formed, though indistinct figure. It was hazy, white, filmy, transparent, a rendering that might have been human. *Might* have.

Charlie studied the series of prints. It was possible to see a head, shoulders, and one arm uplifted as if the specter carried something before it. A form-concealing robe robbed the creature of gender, although it appeared to be slight of build. Jack had changed the camera's location, Charlie realized. These photos were of the upstairs corridor rather than the massive staircase and entrance hall.

"She seems to be hurrying down the passage," Charlie remarked, noting the distances traveled in each photograph.

Jack whisked the proof sheet from her fingers. "She? What makes you think it's female?"

Charlie blinked at him. "I don't know," she said in wonder. "I did say *she*, though." Her brow wrinkled in thought. She chewed her bottom lip. "A feeling. Now, *that's* weird."

"Not so much. In your absence I shared these with the believers. Each identified our ghostly visitor as Mary Mac-Crimmon Douglas. Apparently Mary had a lover and her husband wasn't a man to share. He hacked the man to death, then ran his wife through for good measure."

"Nice guy," Charlie said.

"Now, look at this," Jack handed her another sheet of photos.

Charlie whistled softly between her teeth.

"Yeah," Jack agreed. "It took me that way, too."

The tiny prints followed the pale shade of Mary Mac-Crimmon, each figure getting smaller as the distance between the camera and the form increased. In the first the hall was vacant except for the ghost. Then a man's very solid form entered the corridor from one of the rooms. He was joined by a woman in a negligee, her pale gold hair sweeping her waist as it hung loose over her shoulders. The man pressed her close, his mouth claiming hers in a passionate embrace.

"Don and Gwen!" Charlie breathed. "They cover well. I never guessed."

Jack's finger stabbed at the pictures. "Mary doesn't care for it though."

It was true. The specter grew in density and pushed between the cousins. They separated, puzzled expressions on their faces showing clearly in the light from Gwen's open door. Then, as suddenly as it had appeared in the time-lapse photos of the first page she'd studied, the figure was gone, leaving Don and Gwen in the dim hall alone.

"They made no bones about the pix," Jack commented. "Both claim they saw Mary, and felt her actually shove them apart."

"But do we believe them?" Charlie insisted.

"Yeah," he said. "I do."

She grinned. "Jack, you begin to sound like one of the believers."

He took both proof sheets and stared at them solemnly a moment, arms resting on his thighs as he leaned forward. "You want to hear something crazy? After these pictures, I really *am* beginning to believe."

Charlie was stunned. "You can't actually believe there are such things as ghosts. Don and Gwen could have staged the whole thing. Granted, I don't know how, but they are the ones who got NAB involved, and us."

He shook his head. "No, it isn't their part that convinced

me. This did." He handed her the original sheet of proofs. "Here, where she first appears."

Charlie considered the picture carefully. The camera once again had recorded the time of each shot. At 3:15 A.M. the wide-angle lens had shown a long corridor with a number of doors, all closed, diminishing toward the stairwell. Mary, the specter, stood before the first door, the faint shadow of a smile on her indistinct features.

"I don't get it. She seems pleased about something. Maybe that's the door of her lover's room," Charlie suggested.

Jack made a derisive sound. "You aren't very observant, Chuck. It isn't her anniversary walk. She put in this appearance for a reason."

"The cousins' love affair. Probably, if I follow your current theory, the reason for the uproar. Mary trying to end the connection. Why, I don't know. They are distant cousins."

Jack nodded but stabbed a violent finger at the proof sheet. "Look at the table, the portrait on the wall!"

Charlie didn't understand his insistence. The blank expression in her eyes unnerved him.

"Damn it, Chuck, that is *this* room, *your* room, she's so tickled about! Doesn't that bother you?"

She did him the honor of scrutinizing his photographs once more. The slow, negative movement of her head set her copper ringlets quivering. "I don't see it, Jack. The whole setup is supposed to convince me, but it doesn't."

"But you could be in danger, Chuck. How many more pictures does it take? I'll enlarge these. I'll . . ."

"Nope," Charlie insisted. "You can't convince me it isn't a very clever ruse, Jack. Anything else come up while I was gone?"

Reluctantly, he replaced the proofs in one of the two file folders he'd brought into her room. "Becky brought this out late this afternoon. She said you'd asked for the information pronto."

The knowledge that she'd forgotten the importance of the assignment hung unsaid between them. In the last few years spontaneity had not been part of Charlie's character. The girl who'd eloped with Phil Wilson believed in making decisions on the spur of the moment. Perhaps that girl wasn't completely lost, as she'd believed.

"What is it?" she asked, flipping the folder open. A photocopy of a newspaper photograph of Mark and a stunning brunette stared at her. "*Local racing baron weds,*" bold print below the smiling couple read. "*Pictured are Mark MacCrimmon and his bride, the former Farley Garrison of Garrison Ranch, New Mexico.*"

Charlie snapped the folder shut. It was thick. She knew it contained information about every member of the family and Katrine Rinehart. But it was Farley MacCrimmon's breathtaking features that now burned in her mind with painful detail. She closed her eyes momentarily and still Farley's wide eyes, determined chin, and pouting lips smirked at her.

Charlie opened her eyes to see a worried expression on Jack's familiar features.

He read the turmoil that brewed behind the forced smile she gave him. "I read it," he said. "They were divorced years ago. She ran off with some foreign prince."

The emerald silk of her dress rustled as Charlie shrugged her slim shoulders. "I'm sure it doesn't concern the assignment, or me, Jack." There was an unaccustomed tightness in her throat though.

"Let's join everyone downstairs," Charlie said, making a supreme effort to sound cheerful. "Mrs. MacLynn will be announcing dinner soon."

"Sure," Jack agreed and followed her from the room, leaving the two disturbing folders on the sofa. If she insisted on being blind to possible harm from the spirits he now believed in wholeheartedly, he'd just have to watch out for her. Hell,

Charlie needed someone to protect her. Even if she didn't think so. Damn that independent streak of hers!

Gwen took Charlie's arm the moment she entered the lounge. "I don't think you've met our latest set of ghost hunters," she said. Her gray eyes gleamed with excitement. They nearly sparked. Gwen's voice had a musical lilt that had been missing earlier. Charlie hadn't noticed the woman display any overt emotion before, just well-bred manners. What animated Gwen Hale? Was it the additional players in her little promotional stunt or the successful duping of the cameras last night with a display of violence by her shadow ancestor?

It was still puzzling that the manipulation of props by Gwen and Don had convinced Jack that ghosts did tread the halls of MacCrimmon Manor. Charlie was not as susceptible to their play acting. She had no intention of allowing Gwen to think her act of the evening before had not succeeded though. Perhaps if they believed her a convert as well, the MacCrimmons would slip up.

Charlie smiled at Gwen. "Things do seem to be accelerating, I understand," she commented. "I'd like to interview you and Don on camera later. I hope talking about what happened last night doesn't disturb you. Or the fact that we'll want to use the pictures."

Gwen glowed. "Not in the least."

"What about adverse publicity for Don's campaign?"

"We don't think it will be adverse."

To Charlie it sounded more and more like the MacCrimmons were taking her for a sucker. Well, they'd soon find she wasn't as gullible as her cameraman. It was still strange that Jack had fallen for the carefully staged visitation.

Gwen led Charlie over to where Bill Wynstand was talking with a willowy young man with narrow-rimmed glasses. Wynstand had refilled his brandy snifter and was laughing at something the other had said.

"Two to one! Whadda you think I am? A rube? It's a sure thing!" Wynstand declared. "Ah, the devastating Miss Arden. You did quite right in bringing her straight to me, Gwennie. Did you know that the legendary wife of Merlin, Arthur's court magician, is named Gwendolyn?" he asked Charlie with mock seriousness.

"Who was also legendary wasn't he?" she countered. "Rather appropriate that Merlin's consort should be as well."

"I didn't realize you knew each other," Gwen said with a velvety hostess smile.

"Met in the hall," Wynstand explained. "You haven't met my associate though, Charlie. This is Neil Lovell, a colleague of mine at Duke University. I understand you put in an order for him."

Lovell smiled self-consciously. The thick lenses of his aviator glasses magnified his amber-toned eyes giving them the stark intensity of an image in a Greek Orthodox icon. The illusion was further enhanced by his halo of wispish light brown hair. He sipped at his drink, a screwdriver.

"Wyn's been singing your praises, Miss Arden," he declared as Gwen left them.

"I don't understand his last comment though," Charlie said, taking the hand thrust in her direction. Lovell shook hands energetically. "I don't recall asking for you, Mr. Lovell."

"Oh, not by name, Miss Arden. By profession. I'm a parapsychologist."

"Ahh." Her smile was genuinely pleased now. "I did place an order for one of those. Have you heard much about the spirit activity encountered here at the manor lately?"

"I'm thrilled with it." He almost bounced with enthusiasm. "And to have a chance to work with Katrine Rinehart, as well, is like a fantasy come true."

"Kat Rinehart?" Charlie was astonished to find him eager to work with the medium. She'd mentally put the woman down as a fake. She glanced across the room to where Kat, in another black gown, was eying the new arrivals.

"Certainly," Lovell continued. "Katrine Rinehart is one of our foremost psychics. Fortunately, she's consented to a séance tonight."

Inwardly, Charlie groaned at the prospect.

"On that note," said a mocking voice at her side, "you'll need this." Mark was immaculately groomed once more in a brown tweed jacket, dark silk shirt, loosely knotted tie, and wool slacks.

Charlie accepted the glass of white wine Mark handed her. His eyes raked her boldly, making the specter of Farley Garrison fade from the foreground of Charlie's mind.

"Did you know," Wynstand inquired, "that MacCrimmon means son of the bent one? That Mark means war-like one? That Charlie, or rather Charlene, is a variation of Caroline and means, aptly, a perfect woman, nobly planned? Did you know that I couldn't find a listing for MacLynn in the handy little book from which I gleaned this information in your library?"

Mark sipped at his whiskey. "I wondered from where this fount of knowledge sprang."

"There once was a MacLean, an Irishman, part of the clan of a thirteenth-century Gillean of the Battle-Ax," Wynstand continued.

"Won't wash," Mark said. "You'll never make a limerick rhyme with that one. What, may I ask, brings this on anyway?"

Wynstand waved his glass in the direction of the double doors. "She's looking for someone."

The tiny form of Mrs. MacLynn was indeed on the threshold. She stood on tiptoe peering into the room.

"Excuse me," Mark murmured and melted from Charlie's side. She watched him bend to listen to what the housekeeper excitedly relayed.

114

Charlie turned back to the two men from Duke University. "Another séance, Mr. Lovell? I hope you heard about the failure last night."

He nodded. "Yes, but I'm optimistic. This one will be successful. After all, we have a specter with a mission now. As well as the message last night that someone would return to contact us."

"There was Neal or Niall of the Nine Hostages who died in A.D. 919," Bill Wynstand mused.

Charlie grinned at him. "Another of your spur-of-the-moment research projects? Or are you just determined to change the subject from ghosts, Dr. Wynstand?"

"Actually," the blond man said. "I *am* a professor of medieval history, as Neil can attest. But it is damned impossible to work my field into the normal cocktail conversation."

"I imagine it is," she agreed.

"And I'm under orders," he added. "No ghost talk before dinner."

Deprived of his subject, Lovell took a sudden interest in Kat Rinehart's signals and excused himself.

Charlie's blue eyes widened. "Orders? Whose?"

"Mine, naturally," Mark claimed, rejoining them. "I told him . . ."

". . . no fondling the antiques . . ." Wynstand intoned.

". . . or ghost talk . . ."

". . . or flirting with the redhead . . ."

"Especially that," Mark said and poked his friend in the chest. "You're a married man with two kids. Besides, your wife would kill me if she found out."

Wynstand nodded sadly. "It's a dog's life I lead, fair charmer."

Charlie laughed. "I can see it is. Poor fellow. Care to tell me all about it?"

"No, he doesn't," Mark said. "But he can show you pictures of the family. I have to see Tierney a moment about stable business. I'll be back as soon as I'm able."

"She's in good hands," Wynstand assured him. "As you know I have an extensive collection of snapshots in my wallet."

Mark looked pained. "I know," he moaned and left them.

Wynstand urged Charlie to the bar, where he could refuel his snifter. He offered to refresh her untouched glass of wine.

"So, how long have you known Mark?" he asked.

"Three days." She grinned wryly, surprised that it had been such a short time. It seemed like she'd known him forever, and yet there was so much she didn't know about him. "I should be asking you that question, Dr. Wynstand."

"Bill, remember? Mark and I were at school together. Prep and college. He's a great guy."

Charlie sipped her wine to avoid addressing that statement. What could she say, anyway? That Mark was kind, loving, intoxicating, passionate . . . . "I suppose you knew his wife," she said.

"Farley? Yeah, the ex. Don't worry about her, Charlie. She was no loss."

"You didn't like her?"

"None of us did. She was a gold digger. Only Mark didn't see it."

"And?"

Wynstand's blue eyes twinkled. "She got what she wanted. Forget her. The damage was done and over with long ago."

"What damage?" she pursued.

"You really don't know," Wynstand said, suddenly serious. "Listen, Charlie, if Mark didn't tell you, maybe I shouldn't."

"Shouldn't tell me what?"

He leaned heavily on the gleaming bar top, studying the

brandy in his glass. "It's what they call a need-to-know basis in the service. Maybe he doesn't think you need to know the past."

Charlie set her drink down and traced the edge of the crystal with her finger. "But what do *you* think, Bill?"

"Me?" Wynstand turned on the bar stool to consider her. "I think you should."

"So tell me."

He sighed. "It's a long, boring story."

"I've got the time."

He was silent a moment, gathering his thoughts. Then he spoke in a low-pitched voice to insure they wouldn't be overheard.

"Mark and I go back a long way. And he was always a little crazy when it came to horses. For the rest of us, it was cars and girls. But for Mark, horses. He was single-minded in his pursuit of a better breed of racers. When he met Carl Garrison at a sale, the two of them hit it off. Garrison invited Mark to his ranch, and after that Mark spent every vacation out there working as one of the hands, learning everything Garrison could teach him.

"The year we got our B.A.'s, Farley came home from finishing school. She latched onto Mark immediately."

Wynstand paused to look at the silent young woman. She was staring into her wine, her attitude that of a casual listener. When she glanced up, meeting his eyes, he noticed that the luminous sapphire of her's had deepened with anxiety. She seemed undecided about something. But Charlie's voice was steady as she asked him to continue.

"Farley never cared for Mark, just what the MacCrimmon name brought. She wanted an entry into higher society. She had money and looks, but no class. The first chance she got to "step up"—in her terms—she dumped him for some blue-blood Italian.

"Mark took it badly. He disappeared for months and

finally surfaced as a private in the army with orders for Nam."

Charlie chewed her bottom lip in concentration. "A private? I thought a degree meant officer status."

Wynstand's head inclined slightly. "Not when you're bent on self-destruction. He signed in as a former cowhand from New Mexico."

"But he survived."

"Mark did more than that. It didn't take long to get over Farley once he was in the jungle waiting to get shot. In the end, he pulled four other guys, including the officer of his unit, out of a tight spot. That was just before the U.S. pulled out entirely. When he came back, he buried himself here at MacCrimmon." Wynstand paused and took a pull on his brandy. "Don't get the idea he's been a recluse. There's been a procession of beauties on his arm. None serious. All transient."

As I am, Charlie thought. Not that she'd meant to even let things go as far as they had. Her world and Mark's were nothing alike. They couldn't mix. For all his love of a simple life and hard work, he was still a member of the moneyed class.

Wynstand worried about the bleak look that briefly crossed her lovely face.

"See," he declared with a forced grin, "none of it's worth worrying about."

Her lips curved politely. "Thank you for telling me, Bill."

He raised his glass. "Let's drink to it, Charlie. The past, may it rest forgotten . . . except for the Dark Ages."

Charlie smiled in earnest at his closing quip. "And to medieval historians," she agreed, touching her goblet to his.

"That makes me sound ancient," Wynstand insisted. "I'm not, and here are those pictures of my kids to prove it." He pulled a wallet from the inner pocket of his suit jacket and presented her with a foldout of gangly schoolboys, then paused.

"The need-to-know philosophy works both ways, Charlie," he said seriously. "I think you owe him something in return."

She nodded, yet the shadow in Charlie's eyes remained. Even when Mark returned to find her laughing over photographs of Wynstand's boat, it faded, but did not disappear.

Chapter Seven

THE SETTING WAS the same as the previous séance, though the number of people had increased with the addition of the two men from Duke University. Neil Lovell walked the hall, rubbing his hands together. He mumbled words that sounded suspiciously unscientific. His own equipment lay scattered about the heavy table, much to the annoyance of Jack, who was trying to set up his own cameras and sound system. Kat sat apart from the others, eyes closed, absorbed in her inner thoughts.

Charlie had slipped off after dinner to study the files from the television station. They had confirmed Lovell's statement about Kat Rinehart's credentials. She'd been involved in numerous experiments, had accompanied ghost-hunting writers to allegedly haunted homes, conjured up messages from the dead on both sides of the Atlantic, even assisted the police in solving puzzling crimes. All without the least breath of scandal.

If Kat were on the level and the MacCrimmons weren't, it would explain the séance's failure the evening before. They could be using her as a dupe, a cover. If so, tonight's séance could be a wasted evening. On the other hand, there might be a manifestation or a message.

Either way, Charlie had to find her story soon. The

deadline was approaching and she was still no further along than she had been three days ago when she and Jack had arrived.

Correction. She did have Jack's pictures and footage of one séance, as well as a few interviews. But what tied these things together? How was she to prove there are no such things as ghosts? It *had* to be a plot on the part of the Mac-Crimmon family to generate publicity prior to Don's political announcement.

She had forced herself to include Mark as a participant in the ghost sham. His show of belief in the spirits, and his efforts to convince her of their existence, labeled him as a cohort. In a ruthless moment, she told herself his interest in her was part of the plot, designed to throw her off any scent.

From the Rinehart stories in the file, she'd passed on to clippings regarding the three MacCrimmon cousins and Farley Garrison MacCrimmon. There were also a number of articles showing Mark with a different beauty on his arm for each affair, including a pretty woman jockey.

Wynstand's story, it turned out, had given her a much better picture of Mark than any of the sketchy articles. It enabled her to read between the lines, to see a man who held himself aloof from involvement with the opposite sex, protecting himself from further pain or chance of rejection. Of course, she only had Wynstand's opinion of Mark's emotions concerning Farley's desertion. The photos showed two people in love, a fairy-tale marriage. The divorce had been quiet. Two lines in small print announced that papers had been filed, then later, granted. Another article from a society column noted that MacCrimmon had been decorated for meritorious service and was returning to Louisville. Angus MacCrimmon's sudden death rated three clippings.

None of it had put her any closer to completing her assignment.

"Any on-camera comments, Chuck?" Jack asked, bringing her out of her reverie and back to the chilly, shadowed main hall of MacCrimmon Manor.

Charlie shook her head. "I'll add them later."

"Christ, it's eerie in here," Wynstand said, briskly rubbing his arms. "Cold as a tomb."

Mark saw Charlie shiver and peeled off his jacket, draping it over her thinly clad shoulders. "It is also the oldest part of the house. You should eat it up, Wyn. You're the historian."

Wynstand shrugged. "Can I help it if I like creature comforts?"

Thankful for the warming weight of Mark's tweed jacket, Charlie pulled the garment closer, reveling in the smell of aftershave that clung to it. The scent wrapped her in a cocoon of desire. Every time she smelled the heady fragrance, she knew she would be transported to the private world of passion she had shared with Mark at the cabin. Soon she'd be back in the newsroom, in her own apartment, spending her evenings with a book or the latest network sitcom. There would be no Mark MacCrimmon to disturb her carefully ordered existence, no familiar masculine scent to wreak havoc on her senses.

He had been wrong that first night when he suggested that a capitulation to passion would clear the air and make it easier for them to go about their business. It had had the opposite effect on her. Perhaps due to the celibacy she'd imposed on herself, in the last few years, intimacy with Mark had only made her hunger for his touch more.

For Mark, Charlie suspected that the attraction was fleeting. The folder of pictures showed that he had kept his romantic entanglements short and sweet. Farley had destroyed his capacity for love, just as Charlie had thought Phil had taken hers and thrown it away.

"You expect anything to happen?" Wynstand asked.

"You want out?" Mark countered.

"Not me, buddy boy," Wynstand said. "Wouldn't want to miss Lovell in action."

Mark and Wynstand remained standing on either side of Charlie like a couple of bodyguards. When she moved, they moved. She intercepted a gesture Jack made at Mark, followed by a slight nod. That was curious. Last night Mark had tried to tell her something about the specters, and now Jack believed in them.

Neil Lovell ran a hand through his hair and glanced at the meters on various boxes surrounding the table. "I'm ready to begin if everyone will please take their seats," he said.

Katrine opened her eyes and smiled gently at Lovell. Her thin hands stretched outward on the table. "Dr. Lovell. Mark," she whispered, indicating the chairs on either side of her. Her eager, puppy-dog looks were now directed at Lovell, Charlie noted, rather than at the MacCrimmon men. And Lovell seemed to respond to Kat's fervent smile.

Taking the chair Mark held for her, Charlie found herself sandwiched between him and Wynstand. Don and Gwen took the remaining straight-backed chairs. Expertly kicking cords from his path, Jack circled the table, the lightweight video camera balanced on his shoulder.

With an admiring Lovell holding her hand, Kat achieved her trance state quickly. Linette's taste differed from the medium's however, for when Kat's eyes opened once more, she stared invitingly at Mark. *"Bon jour,"* she said in a husky Parisian voice.

"Hello, Linette," the laird greeted. "Nice to see you. Bring anyone with you tonight?"

Lovell bristled at his host's levity. "Please." His voice, a harsh whisper, hissed in the lofty chamber, echoing repeatedly. "For the sake of science, at least allow me to conduct the proceedings."

Mark's dark eyes hardened. He seemed ready to object,

but instead he allowed the parapsychologist to guide the séance.

Under the table, Mark's knee pressed against Charlie's and once again, memories of their tangled bodies invaded her thoughts. Her need for him, carefully banked since their return to the manor, swept over Charlie, leaving her flushed under the now smoldering gleam in Mark's eyes.

"Is there someone who wishes to contact us this evening, Linette?" Lovell asked, bringing Charlie's attention back to the proceedings. He leaned forward in the hard chair, his face radiating enthusiasm rather than scholarly interest.

"*Oui.*"

"A name."

"Crimmon," she murmured. "A piper?"

"The MacCrimmons were the MacLeods' pipers on the Isle of Skye," Wynstand said. The information earned him a scowl from Lovell.

Kat's face broke into a smile of understanding; her head tilted to one side and turned as if she were listening to someone at her shoulder. "A lady. She longs for a piper."

Lovell cast a thunderous look at the other participants, daring them to volunteer information and thus disrupt the scientific purpose of the séance.

"The cry of pipes," Linette rambled.

"A lady," Lovell repeated. "Does she have a name, a first name? What does she wish us to call her?"

"Lady Dou . . . no. Mary."

Too convenient, Charlie thought. Everyone identifies Jack's spirit photos of the previous night as Mary MacCrimmon Douglas and she conveniently turns up at the séance, their first visitor from the other side. Charlie glanced appraisingly at each of the MacCrimmon cousins. Seated next to Lovell, Gwen was also leaning toward the table in anticipation of the medium's next words. Her blond hair swung free in a thick curtain about her shoulders, draping over one eye, shielding part of her face. All her attention appeared to be directed at the entranced woman at the head of the table. On her left, Don was not interested in the alleged voice from the grave. His awareness was of his lovely cousin's form, of the way the scooped neckline of her dress gaped away from her breasts as she leaned forward.

Lovell had insisted on checking the table and chairs for hidden devices before they began the séance. Since there had been no sign of alleged poltergeist activity, Charlie had wondered at the need for such preventive measures. Lovell had balked at a physical search of his revered Miss Rinehart, however. The Victorian spiritualists, of whom Charlie had read at the library before coming to MacCrimmon Manor, had been overly fond of noisy, visual demonstrations. Modern psychics seemed to shun manifestations of ectoplasm clinging to their shoulders. And the articles concerning Kat that Charlie had recently read reported messages from the deceased but never a physical visitation.

That didn't mean someone else wouldn't put on a show though. Gwen's full sleeves and flowing gray skirts could conceal tricks. The same could be said of her two male counterparts. Their suits offered as much concealment as a stage magician used for his illusions.

And the fact that Charlie wore Mark's sport coat draped around her shoulders did not clear him of suspicion, either.

"Is Mary troubled, Linette?" Lovell asked.

"Aye, I am that, mon," responded a different voice.

Charlie glanced at the medium, then to the camera to make sure Jack had it trained on the woman. Kat's appearance had changed once more. She had released the hands of the men on either side of her and now half stood, leaning on the heels of her hands, bracing her weight against the table. The woman who looked out of Kat's pale eyes was no longer timid, was no longer casting Linette's seductive, melting glances. These eyes radiated determination, a sense of command. "Troubled, ye say? With the clan reduced ta a pitiful state by our enemies? Ye ken the straights the MacDonalds have stripped us ta?"

It was Wynstand's turn to strain forward. "What year is it, my lady?" he demanded, his eyes glowing in the firelight.

"Year? Year?" Mary bellowed. "The year of disaster, mon. The MacDonalds raided, took our cattle, kilt the bonny laird, stole the lasses. Left us—left me—ta the mercies of the Douglas."

"Are you the lady of the manor, Mary?" Lovell's voice was devoid of emotion, although his countenance was flushed with suppressed excitement.

"The laird's lady? I be his sister. Ah, Owen, how could ye leave me ta this end?"

"What end, Mary?"

"Dinna ye ken, mon? With Owen gone I must raise the bairns. Young Marcus and Donal. The last of their clan." Kat's head dropped on her breast wearily as Mary contemplated the task ahead of her.

Mark shrugged in answer to the silent questions directed at him from around the table. "Just coincidence that the names are similar."

"Shh!" Lovell hissed. He turned back to Kat. "Mary, can you hear me?"

"Aye, aye. I ken, mon. The Douglas was a mistake. I never should have taken him ta spouse when I loved another. But Davy couldna train the young laird. All for the clan. All for nought."

"Why do you think that, Mary?"

The eyes that Mary shared with the personalities of Kat and Linette narrowed. "Dinna ye ken? The young laird resists all brides, and the other covets a MacDonald! Ah, but my Davy has returned. A blessing he is ta me." She sighed. "Something must be done. The clan canna fall inta the Douglas's hands. He's a cruel man in league with the Mac-

Donalds." Determination and pain waged war in her lilting brogue.

"Can't we help her?" Gwen whispered.

"Mary," Lovell said. "All is well. The clan continues."

The medium cast him a disbelieving, glowering look. "And who be ye? By the sound of yer voice, not a Highland mon. Not a clansman."

"A friend," the parapsychologist insisted.

Mary dismissed him with a wave of Kat's hand, narrowly missing clawing his nose with the medium's lacquered nails.

"He speaks true," Gwen said softly. "The clan continues, Mary."

"Nay, lass. The manor na rings with the laughter o' bairns."

"Laird Marcus wed and produced five strong sons over three hundred years ago," Gwen insisted.

Mary sank back into the chair wearily. "'Tis not then of which I speak. The blood is weak. I pray ye, lass, dinna be taintin' it."

Charlie could feel tension building in Mark. She sensed it in the grip of his hand and the pressure of his knee on hers. When he finally spoke, she wasn't surprised to hear his voice, or the command in his tone.

"There is nothing you can do anymore, Mary. What transpires will be left to fate. Do you understand?"

"I ken."

"Return Katrine to us."

"Aye." She laid her hands flat on the table and closed her eyes. "I will mind the fey one," she said.

"Damn," Mark muttered under his breath and glanced at Charlie, again squeezing her hand.

She was puzzled by the intensity of his look.

Then his gaze shifted in quick succession to Wynstand and Jack. It was as if a silent message passed between the three men. What sort of message? A signal? If so, how *was* Jack involved?

At the head of the table, Kat's breathing was deep and even. When her eyes fluttered open it was not the medium but the control who addressed the table. "Another wishes to speak," she said.

Lovell was in his element with Linette. His hand found Katrine's pulse and measured it carefully. "Katrine should not be possessed again, Linette. Is there a message?"

"*Oui.*"

"Is it for a particular person? Or for all of us?"

"For the laird."

Beside her, Charlie heard Mark utter an obscenity.

"From whom is the message?"

"Angus." Kat's head tilted to the right. She looked at a point on the table before Mark. "He prefers . . . a *franc* for his pride."

"I know he does," Mark said. "But we'll do things my way."

"You understand the message?" Lovell demanded.

"It's about horses," Don said. "Pride is the name of a colt."

"He says the filly is bonny and will breed well," Linette continued.

"Tell him to buzz off," Mark snapped.

"Katrine tires," Linette pointed out. The medium dropped in the chair, despite the animation Linette's personality lent to her pale, pinched face.

"Return her to us," Lovell asked politely. "Thank you for your assistance this evening, Linette."

Charlie felt weary herself. It was as if energy were draining from her limbs. Her hand was warm where it touched Mark's, but an icy-cold draft had penetrated the warmth of his jacket, making her shiver. Thank goodness the séance was ending. She could sit next to a blazing fire and collect her thoughts. She had to impose some order on the interviews, pictures, and film clips, or else she'd never meet her deadline. Whether she believed in ghosts or not, the story was perfect for Halloween. However, it was difficult to put her feelings for Mark aside and view her work objectively.

It was strange that Charlie always caught such a chill at these séances. Wynstand's earlier remark about the manor was true. The hall was a cold, drafty, thoroughly uncomfortable place. Impossible to live in, yet fascinating. She would miss it when she left. It was easy to get used to the luxury of MacCrimmon Manor. She wondered if Jack felt the same about the place. The setting alone probably accounted for his sudden conversion to belief in the MacCrimmon shades.

She watched as Jack taped the medium's return to reality, occasionally sweeping the seated participants with the camera's eye. They would have to edit the film together.

The alleged specter of Mary MacCrimmon Douglas had started out reliving the events that led to her death, then swung clearly to the present. Even if one actually believed Mary was a voice from the grave, the abrupt change in time was still puzzling. As a nonbeliever, Charlie made a mental note to track down a written or verbal account of this MacCrimmon ancestress, and of the nephews whose names corresponded so closely with their present descendants. With so many Scottish families working at the manor and stable, a legend was sure to have survived. The film could be cut at the point when Lovell had requested Kat Rinehart's return. Obviously they didn't need the last cryptic comments concerning the stable. . . . Damn, it was cold!

The minicam had swung past her to continue its sweep back to the medium when suddenly Jack brought it back in Charlie's direction, the omniscient single lens trained on her. In the same moment Mark pulled Charlie from her chair, dragging her away from the table with Wynstand following him in blind confusion.

Lovell jumped from his chair before recalling that he still held Kat's limp wrist between his fingers. "What the hell . . ."

"Jack," Mark's voice cut over the parapsychologist's roughly. "Did you see . . .?"

The cameraman stopped the film. "Gone now, but I think I actually got her!"

Mark thrust Charlie into Wynstand's arms. His jacket had fallen from her shoulders so that Charlie shivered as she pushed away from the historian. "What is going on?"

She started forward only to find Wynstand's hand restraining her.

"Not near the table, Charlie," he advised. "Didn't you see anything? Feel anything?" He was pale beneath his ruddy complexion.

She shrugged from beneath his grasp. "What the hell is the matter with everyone?"

No one answered her. Charlie doubted anyone heard her.

Kat returned to full consciousness and blinked at the confusion around her. Lovell was busy checking his instruments. Jack practically ripped the camera open in his eagerness to get at the film. Mark surveyed the room anxiously, his breathing quick. "Damn," he said, exasperated. "I'm too keyed up. I can't tell if they're here yet. Don? Gwen? Anything?"

The two cousins were seemingly the only calm members of the séance. They sat at ease, holding hands openly.

Charlie found herself clasped against the cool silk of Mark's shirt in an embrace that threatened her ribs. "Damn them to hell," he muttered. "Are you all right, Charlie? No after effects?"

She struggled to free herself from his crushing arms. "From what? Has everyone gone mad?"

"The manifestation," Lovell sputtered, still bent over his equipment. "The readings . . ."

"An apparition!" Kat breathed. "But I've never . . ."

"My God, when she reached out to you . . ." Mark growled.

"The cold was arctic . . ." Wynstand shuddered.

"All on film!" Jack crowed. "Christ, I hope it develops as well as the other night's shots."

"I need a drink," Gwen announced, getting to her feet majestically. She swayed, as if her legs refused to support her slight weight. Don's arm went protectively about her waist.

"What is the matter with everyone?" Charlie demanded loudly. "What manifestation?"

Jack shut his camera. "Mary MacCrimmon Douglas, naturally."

"Where? When?" Charlie snapped. "Did everyone else see her?"

Don and Gwen nodded. Lovell shook his head sadly. Wynstand shuddered and admitted, "I felt something clammy touch my hand."

"She began forming right inside the table before you," Jack claimed, packing his equipment away carefully. He detached the microphone from Mark's collar. "As she gained substance, she reached out to you." Jack's hand performed an instant replay, slowly reaching for her face, then changed direction and plucked the microphone from her dress. "That's when Mark grabbed you away from her."

Charlie found the story impossible. She hadn't seen anything or felt anything like Wynstand described. The reactions of the others were varied as well. Jack was ecstatic, Lovell disgruntled, Kat astounded and pleased, Wynstand obviously frightened, Gwen uneasy, and Don concerned. Mark alone radiated fury. She seemed to be the only member of the party to remain untouched, unaffected by the séance.

The reporter in her came to the forefront, easily taking command. Charlie's voice was firm as she requested them to all stay where they were. "I'd like everyone's reactions on film."

At her side Mark nodded curtly. "In the lounge," he suggested. "We all need a drink."

The fire jumped erratically, responding to gusts of wind that howled about the chimneys heralding a change in the weather. No shadows danced tonight, however. By unspoken agreement all the lamps in the room glowed. The eight men and women gathered before the fireplace all held tumblers of bourbon. Mark hadn't asked for preferences, he'd just poured and handed them each a glass. The alcohol dimmed their inhibitions so that they were less aware of the camera as it caught and recorded their every word and expression.

"It was almost like a hologram," Jack explained during his turn before the lens. "She wasn't a flat image nor single surfaced. She was three dimensional and yet transparent, colorless."

"No, her hair was a deep auburn," Gwen said. "And she wore it loose."

"I thought I smelled heather just before the materialization," Don contributed. "But I could be wrong."

"The cold was intense," Wynstand insisted. "Clammy."

Neil Lovell kept his cassette recorder rolling in unison with Charlie's interviews. "I registered a distinct drop in temperature, but didn't see anything myself. Just the violent reactions of Mr. MacCrimmon and Dr. Wynstand," he said, acutely conscious of the camera.

"Is there a scientific explanation as to why an apparition was seen by only some of the participants?" Charlie asked.

"None." Lovell sighed. "There are many theories on why it is possible to even experience manifestations. The blood ties the MacCrimmons and Ms. Hale have in common with the spirit could account for their ability to see her. It doesn't explain Mr. Donahue's ability unless there is an unknown blood connection with the family. Energy from the living can be used by a spirit to build a visible picture of itself. The living would probably feel very drained or tired, just as a medium often experiences exhaustion through contact with the spirits. Then again, if Mary had merely been reliving the tragic episode of her death, the explanation would be a simple electrical imprint on the stone of the manor."

Lovell pushed his glasses straight on the bridge of his nose. "At this time, I couldn't say, Ms. Arden. It's a link with the past to be able to see the forms of men and women who lived centuries ago, in a country several thousand miles away."

"Tell me more about this electrical imprint," she urged. "Just what is it?"

"The majority of hauntings are due to a violent act. Often the death of the person appearing. The trauma, fear, emotion, if you will, expended at such a time is a type of electrical energy. It imprints just as your film does. The image or event is recorded on the surroundings. In this case, on the stonework of the manor. What occured in the past happened within these walls even though the manor was then situated in the Highlands of Scotland."

"So when Jane Steele married James MacCrimmon and brought the house to Kentucky in 1921, she also brought the imprints or memories?"

"That's right."

"But during her trance, Miss Rinehart uttered messages that were definitely not a reenactment of a past event," Charlie pursued.

Lovell smiled. "That is a separate case. Verbal communication through the intercession of a medium rarely has its basis in the imprint theory."

"So it is just a theory, not a factual scientific statement, Dr. Lovell?"

Lovell's grin widened. "We're trying, Miss Arden. That's why I'm here."

Charlie sighed and made a cutting motion at her partner behind the camera. "We're going in circles," she muttered. "It's giving me a headache."

Jack stretched and yawned. "Let's call it a night. I'll

develop everything so you can view it in the morning, Chuck. Just wait till you see our ghost. Then things will sort themselves out."

Charlie rubbed the back of her neck in an effort to relieve the building tension. "I doubt it, but perhaps you're right, Jack. Go on. Get some sleep."

Don and Gwen had left sometime earlier, assisting a drained Kat Rinehart to her room. Now Lovell and Wynstand trailed Jack and his camera out the door.

Outside the tall, narrow windows, the sharp tattoo of rain began. A few flashes of lightning and crashes of thunder were all the evening needed to fit into the script of a hundred horror movies. Within a few minutes, however, the wind dropped, taking the ferocity of the torrent with it. The gentle hush of drops against the windowpanes was soothing rather than terrorizing. It did not ease the tension that had been building within Charlie.

She sat forward on the hassock she'd pulled up before the roaring fire. Amber lights danced in the sunset-colored curls that spilled over her closed eyes as she massaged the muscles at the base of her neck. "Damn, I'll never make heads or tails of this thing," Charlie muttered.

"Yes, you will," Mark's deep voice said behind her. His large hands replaced hers as he worked the tension from her shoulders. "It isn't the first tough assignment you've had. Or the last."

She laughed shortly. The sound was harsh. "Tough? Try impossible. The network wants to see a finished product early next week and it's already Thursday . . . no, Friday morning. I shouldn't have wasted today. I should have been working."

Mark's lips followed his hands at the nape of her neck. "I'd hardly call it wasted, love."

She turned, apologetic, her sapphire eyes softening. "A poor choice of words."

"Very." he agreed, sliding one arm around her slim waist while the other continued stroking her back. "But I understand. You can't find a story because you don't believe in my ghosts."

"Mmm," she murmured, leaning back sleepily against his broad, muscled chest. "I don't. I didn't see anything. Didn't feel anything out of the ordinary and didn't smell anything different."

"Nothing?" he asked against her hair.

"Well," she purred, "maybe your cologne. It's very distracting."

"Is it now?"

"Mmm." She was content to rest in the comfort of his arms and feel the gentle touch of his hands dispelling tension.

Charlie's head fell back against Mark's shoulder. His lips brushed light kisses on her temples, then on her gently smiling lips. He continued to knead her back.

"Mmm," she sighed once more. "That feels so good. I could stay here forever."

"Why don't you?"

She didn't take him seriously. From the offhanded way Mark said it, Charlie knew he didn't mean it. "Can't. I have—" his lips silenced her temporarily as he planted two more teasing, soft kisses on her mouth "—a story to put together."

"Then how about for a very short night?"

"With you?" She grinned mischievously, her eyes reflecting the dancing firelight. "What could you possibly have in mind?"

"I'm self-sacrificing," he said. "I was thinking only of your need to relax." He gave her a wicked smile.

"How thoughtful. And just how do you propose to ease my tension?"

He nibbled lightly on her earlobe and worked his way

down the expanse of creamy white throat to where the high collar of her dress prohibited further exploration. "I have a few ideas," he admitted.

"I'll bet you have."

"Starting with a massage and then . . ."

"Mmm. Sounds delicious. You shouldn't tempt me, though." She sat up reluctantly. "I've got a lot of work to do tomorrow. I'd better get to bed."

"That's exactly what I had in mind."

"I know you did." She smiled and twisted out of his arms to face him on the ottoman. "But I can't."

"Can't or won't?"

"Either. I'm not on vacation. I have a job to do."

Mark's raven brows arched. "I thought we'd put all that behind us."

The harshness of his voice put Charlie on the defensive. "All what? My better judgment?" She shrugged off his hands. The truce had only been temporary then, she thought. He was still a chauvinist who thought she'd be eager to jump in his bed at the wink of an eye. It didn't matter that she wanted to do just that. She had to pull herself back together, to keep herself free from one-sided emotional commitments such as this. The women in his life were one-night stands. Passing fancies. Only his libido was involved, not his heart. Yet in just a few short days, she had fallen in love with Mark MacCrimmon. Had broken every promise she'd made to herself five years ago. Had given in to her desires. Had dared to dream.

Midnight had come and gone now, and Cinderella didn't fit in at the palace anymore. The enchantment was just that: an enchantment, an illusion.

"Better judgment!" Mark sputtered. "Is that what you call it? What's your plea for your slip this afternoon, then? Temporary insanity?"

"Yes," she countered, equally angry now. "That's exactly

what it was. I was insane to try things your way!" She was also insane to stay so near him when she wanted him so badly.

"My way!" he growled. "If that doesn't take the cake, sister. You wanted me as much as I wanted you."

Charlie tried with difficulty to keep her voice under control. She wanted to shriek at him. She wanted to storm from the room, slamming the door in his arrogant, masculine face. She wanted to show him there was one woman he couldn't trifle with as he had the various women in the newspaper clippings. She wanted to throw herself in his arms and babble that she couldn't live without him. But she could live without him. And would.

Her chin came up, determined. "I wasn't the one who preached that to remove a distraction, you capitulated to lust. 'Get it out of our systems,' you said. Well, I have!"

"I haven't."

"That's your problem."

"*Our* problem, sweetheart," he ground out, furious. "That appetizer this afternoon just whet my appetite for the full course."

Charlie got to her feet. Her breast rose and fell rapidly as her temper accelerated. She fought to regain control. "Good night, Mr. MacCrimmon," she said, the words nearly choking her. She marched to the door.

Mark's pursuit was lightning-fast. Before she had taken two strides, his hand fell like a band of iron on her arm, spinning her to face the danger in his black eyes.

"You aren't walking out on me that easily, you little liar. You feel the same way I do."

"Correction. I did. I've dealt with my lust," she said.

"Like hell." Mark crushed her to him, his lips roughly claiming hers, forcing her mouth to open under his onslaught. Unbidden passion unraveled within her, answering the brutality of his embrace with an insistence of its own. Charlie pressed close to him, molding her body seductively to his, tantalizing him with the taste of victory.

When they parted, desire had replaced the fury in his face. "Charlie . . ." he began, his voice harsh with passion.

Outwardly calm, Charlie stepped away from his arms. "As I said," she declared, her voice icy, "I have dealt with my lust. Since you cannot accept that, I'll leave in the morning. Someone else will be sent to finish the assignment. Good night."

She closed the door softly, managing to retain her dignity during the endless walk down dim corridors to her room. Once there her defenses dropped and, throwing herself on the bed, Louisville's leading lady journalist sobbed hysterically for the man she loved but could never have.

Chapter Eight

MARK LEANED BACK against the couch, one leg propped up, the other stretched out toward the cabin's fireplace. Earlier he had made love to Charlie in front of it.

He drew on his cigarette then stubbed it out in the nearly overflowing ashtray on the floor beside him. For two hours he had stared at the softly glowing coals in the fireplace without really seeing them. Instead he relived the events of the evening, watching again as the specter of Mary Mac-Crimmon Douglas reached out to gently stroke Charlie Arden's cheek.

Damn. Why had Mary done such a thing? And how could Charlie not have seen or felt it?

He lit another cigarette. The only answer lay in Charlie herself. "The fey one" Mary called her. More than merely fey! She was downright maddening.

Not only had she refused the comfort of his bed, she'd made him so furious that he had stormed out of the house and saddled Madoc. The insane, dangerous gallop in the rain cooled his temper. But in its absence he had merely gotten irritated. Not only at Charlie, but at himself for getting soaked.

Now dressed in dry jeans, a towel draped around his bare shoulders, he wished he had not come to the cabin, the scene of their Eden-like Iliad. Here Charlie's image was just as vivid and disturbing as the shades of his ancestors were back at the manor.

Mark sighed. How long had it been since he'd felt this way about any woman? Over fifteen years ago he had made the mistake of falling in love with Farley Garrison. He had not repeated the folly. It was hard to remember the glow of that first love. It certainly was nothing like the need he felt for Charlie Arden. If she hadn't come to the manor hunting for ghosts, his life would have remained well-planned and uncomplicated.

But she had come and Mark doubted seriously that he would ever be the same man he had been before her arrival. Was it love, this tremendous hurt, this feeling that he was incomplete?

Mark pushed the thought aside. What mattered was the threat to Charlie that he saw in the attempt Mary MacCrimmon had made to possess her.

He hadn't wanted to believe it, although he'd watched it all happen. As Kat Rinehart had slowly come out of her trance, Charlie herself had begun to exhibit signs of going into one. She didn't even realize that she had, which really scared him. The trance state was dangerous enough for Kat, a trained psychic. But for Charlie it was psychic suicide. She didn't know what awaited her. He was almost sure that if he hadn't acted when he did, Mary would have taken control of Charlie's unconscious form.

The manor had always been the site of supernatural manifestations. He and Don joked about it, but they had grown up accepting the ghostly phenomena as normal. And of the two brothers, he had been more attuned to the shades of his ancestors, had always known they were there, had always known he had nothing to fear from them.

But he was of the same bloodline. Charlie wasn't.

140

Why had Mary made such a blatant attempt at possession? She hadn't appeared in so long.

Of course the paranormal activity had increased long before Charlie Arden had come to MacCrimmon Manor. It had become more noticeable just after Don had returned home, bringing Gwen with him.

Don's law practice in Lexington was successful. And Gwen's position in public relations with a New York City firm had been a coup of which she had been inordinately proud. He hadn't seen much of either of them the last five years. Then suddenly Don had called, asking if he could move back into the manor while he got established in Louisville again. He was interested in running for the state senate from his hometown. It had been a surprise when Gwen had also turned up and announced she had left her job to work on Don's campaign.

Could it be their love affair that lay at the root of the ghostly occurences? Mary's reaction to Gwen was easily identified. Gwen's father had MacDonald blood. Even centuries later Mary found that untenable. Or had the supernatural activity merely been a stronger concentration of clan blood? With three MacCrimmons in residence, there was an increase in sources from which the spirits could draw energy for visibility.

A long tail of ash dropped from Mark's cigarette to the rug, causing him fresh irritation. Frustrated, he stubbed the butt out and got to his feet. He wasn't getting any closer to the reasons or the truth. It didn't matter any longer why the paranormal activity had increased. The problem had changed. The redirection of spirit energy toward Charlie Arden scared him. And Jack Donahue shared that fear.

He got to his feet and moved across the room to the bed. The bedclothes were still rumpled from earlier in the day. He could still see the imprint of Charlie's head on the pillows.

He needed sleep but doubted it would come. A hint of lavender, her perfume, hung in the air.

Once the cabin had been a refuge. Now the memory of a passionate woman with fire-bright hair haunted it.

Mark dropped on the bed. There would be no sleep this night. He was the trespasser now, for the cabin was no longer his. It belonged to the disturbingly beautiful reporter from Channel 5.

Only the bait of a plum network assignment led Charlie to the track near the stables at dawn. At least, that was what she repeatedly told herself as she trod the sodden ground and braved the damp morning air. Her heart had nothing to do with the decision.

When Stan had first told her of the opportunity to leave Channel 5, she hadn't wanted to entertain the idea. Now, leaving Kentucky seemed the best way to mend the damage done to her heart. Throwing herself into a new job, into new surroundings, would make it possible to forget Mark MacCrimmon. But she had to complete the assignment first, and an apology to Mark for her actions—or was it non-actions?—the night before was in order. Perhaps she could enlist Jack's aid in staying away from their host for the remainder of her stay. Whether any other ghostly encounters occured or not, the story had to be wrapped up by Sunday morning. It should have been completed already.

Sleep had been impossible. She had gone over the information in the folder, and her notes, once more. The proofs of Jack's spirit photos had spurred her thoughts back to the assignment when they threatened to stray to memories of betrayed jet eyes, tender kisses, and strong arms enfolding her.

Mark had been right, unfortunately, in saying she hadn't found her story because she didn't believe in the spirits that haunted MacCrimmon. She'd been trying to disprove the existence of ghosts rather than report on their alleged appearances at the manor. The new perspective made some of the material she had already gathered fall into a slot of sorts. What she needed now was to experience a manifestation herself. If that were possible. It was puzzling that Jack had seen the apparition at the séance and she hadn't—and after everyone insisted it had formed right in front of her. It had tried to touch her. Why had that movement thrown Mark, Wynstand, and Jack into a panic? "Morning, Miss Arden," Tim Tierney greeted her as she reached the track. "Have you seen Mark?"

She shook her head. "No, I'm sorry. Perhaps Mrs. MacLynn . . ."

"Nope. She said his bed at the house hasn't bene slept in. Probably went out to the cabin since Madoc's missing, too. Excuse me."

Charlie had thought to find Bill Wynstand at the track, but the only men gathered were the stable hands she'd seen there the day before, Tierney the trainer, and Jimmy the exercise boy. Prefering not to disrupt their work, Charlie took a place on the rail a little apart from the others and gazed out at Angus's Pride.

The colt was eager to run. He danced on the end of his tether, his long, well-shaped legs kicking up the light covering of mud on the track. The cool morning breeze tossed his mane and paraded his dark tail as he pranced. He snorted, blowing a cloud of vapor. Then, as if recognizing a familiar scent, he sidled toward her. When the rein in Jimmy's hand brought him to a halt, Pride pulled, indicating to the exercise boy that he didn't like standing still. Tierney noticed and told the boy to lead the fidgeting colt around.

Pride hadn't wanted to walk the complete track though. He stopped before Charlie and thrust his muzzle into her gloved hands.

"Good morning, Miss Arden," Jimmy said cheerfully. "Looks like you've made a friend."

Charlie laughed as Pride pushed against her hand. "He just remembers I slipped him some sugar yesterday when no one was looking."

"Yeah? The boss always does that," the boy told her.

"Tierney?" She knew the guess was wrong as soon as she uttered it.

"Naw, Mr. MacCrimmon. Tim says if the horses didn't get a lot of exercise, they'd all have weight problems." His wide smile indicated that it was a running joke around the stable.

Charlie grinned in response. "It must keep you pretty busy, Jimmy."

"Yeah, but I like it." He patted the chestnut's sleek neck. "You here to watch Jaffee up on Pride?"

She had forgotten the jockey was due to arrive that morning. Mark would be busy discussing contracts for the racing season. Chances were she wouldn't be able to talk to him that morning at all. Jimmy's face radiated such eagerness she couldn't disappoint him, though. "Wouldn't miss it," she assured him. "You think Jaffee's a good choice?"

"Well, I think Francie would do a bang-up job riding him. Tim says that's just because I sort of had a crush on her when she worked here. I think she was Tim's first choice, too, only he didn't want to suggest her seein' that she and the boss were . . . er . . . well, I guess I shouldn't be tellin' you that, Miss Arden," he finished in confusion. "It don't matter now. Jaffee's here and I know he can't wait to get astride the Pride. I can tell."

Charlie tried to ignore the implication of a romantic attachment between Mark and the unknown Francie. She concentrated on Nick Jaffee's arrival. "He's here? I didn't see anyone but Tim's staff," she said.

"Oh, he and Francie holed up in Tim's office drinkin' coffee. Said it was too cold to wait for the boss out here when they didn't have to." Jimmy obviously didn't care for the attitude. He proved it with his next statement. "Francie used to be on the track at all hours and in all kinds of weather."

"Don't worry," Charlie soothed. "She's probably just being polite. Who is she, anyway?"

Pride, deprived of the anticipated sugar cube, pulled at the rein again, eager to be off in a different direction. Jimmy quieted him with a few soft words and rubbed the horse's muzzle soothingly. "You don't know Francine Voight, the best female jockey on the program today?"

The name rang a faint bell with her, but she couldn't say why.

"Francie started here just like me, exercising horses," Jimmy declared. "Mr. MacCrimmon gave her her first break as a jockey and helped her get established. She was under contract to the tartan colors till last spring, when she signed to ride for another stable."

If she'd wanted to pursue the conversation about another woman, one who was connected with Mark, the laird's thunderous, theatrical arrival made it impossible at that time. Charlie wasn't sure if she welcomed the interruption.

Moments before he actually reached the track, the patient MacCrimmon employees heard the pounding of the gray's hooves galloping across the meadow. The dark blur on his back was bent low over the animal's neck, unmindful of the mane that whipped his face. Madoc didn't have Pride's speed, but his stride was long and even as the ground fell away from his flying hooves. Mark didn't pull back on the reins until they were almost upon the men at track side. The gray skidded to a halt in the dense mud, then rose on his hind legs to paw the crisp air with his front hooves.

"Very funny," Tierney said dryly. "Jaffee's been here half an hour already."

"Eager bastard, isn't he?" Mark quipped, sliding from the saddle. He murmured in his mount's attentive ear and sent him off to the stable with a gentle slap on the rump. Madoc's large hooves made sucking sounds in the muck as he pranced obediently through the large, open double doors into the warm, aromatic barn. A groom met him at the door, retrieving the trailing reins, and began walking the gelding to cool him down.

Charlie found herself impressed by the docile way the massive horse followed his master's instructions, and the efficiency of the stableman. Mark trained everyone well, from his animals to his employees. Was it any wonder that he reacted so violently when she refused to dance to his tune? The man was accustomed to blind obedience.

"He's got someone with him, Mark. Maybe you should be warned . . ." the trainer began.

"Mark!" a female voice greeted. "I see Madoc hasn't forgotten any of his tricks."

MacCrimmon glanced toward the tiny, dark-haired woman. "Too late," he murmured to Tim. "Francie, what a surprise," he answered the woman.

"A pleasant one, I hope," she said, smiling. "It's been a long time, Mark." She had reached him now, and with a springing jump, had thrown herself into his arms, hugging him with pleasure.

Charlie experienced an intense desire to scratch the woman's eyes out. Her slim hands tightened on the railing, her knuckles turning white with the pressure. What had she expected? A period of mourning before he found more welcoming arms? She'd been right in her original estimation of his personality. He'd never seen her as anything but another conquest.

Then why did she feel betrayed? Why did she recall the firm but gentle touch of his hand, of his lips? Why did memories flash in rapid succession in her mind, showing her the myriad facets of the man? Was Mark the hot-headed barbarian who took what he wanted, or was he the thoughtful romantic into whose arms she'd willingly gone?

Watching Francine Voight embrace Mark was masochistic, Charlie thought. She'd never before recognized the need for self-castration. She'd berated herself over the failure of her marriage to Phil Wilson, but the remembered pain of the past was pale when compared to the rending of her soul as the petite woman continued to cling to Mark's arm. Francine had a proprietary way of smiling at him that further irritated Charlie.

The difference in their heights would have been ridiculous if Francine hadn't been so sure of her position at Mark's side. She was slim and tiny. Her olive complexion was flawless. Two heavy black braids framed her square face, accenting high cheekbones before falling over her breasts to her narrow waist. She wore a short, white ski jacket with skin-tight jeans stuffed into the tops of tall, brown riding boots. Charlie felt pale and insignificant next to the jockey's vibrant looks.

"I came with Nick, naturally," Francine purred up at Mark. "When he told me what was up, nothing could have kept me away."

"Any excuse, huh, Francie?" Mark said.

"Oh, aren't we a bear today?" she teased. "Come meet Nick. I know Tim has worked with him before, but you and he have never officially met, Mark."

Jaffee looked a leprechaun next to Mark's tall frame. Bushy sideburns tried to compensate for the thinning thatch of brown hair beneath the baseball cap the little man wore on the back of his head. There was something about his small eyes and pinched features that made Charlie uneasy.

After introductions were made, Francine skipped under the fence out to the colt in the center of the track. She made a fuss over the smitten exercise boy before running knowing hands along Pride's glistening coat.

The two men stood apart from the chestnut's handlers and watched the tiny woman as she examined the colt with loving care.

"Fine-looking horse," Jaffee complimented. "And he hasn't run yet?"

"Worried that he's not up to your standards?" Mark snapped.

The jockey side-stepped. "I'm not fool enough to doubt a MacCrimmon breed. Anyway, Francie is convinced he's a winner. That's enough for me."

"Francie's prejudiced," Mark said. "But let's see what you can do. Just hand ride him once around the track."

Jaffee's eyes narrowed as he looked the dancing colt over. "I'd like to feel what he can do, MacCrimmon. Trottin' won't tell me what I want to know."

"Once around easy, Jaffee," Mark repeated, uncompromising.

"Sure. Once," the little man agreed.

"Leave the stick, Jaffee. Pride doesn't need any encouragement to run."

Jaffee looked down at the riding crop he carried with military precision beneath his arm. "It's sort of a talisman, MacCrimmon. A rabbit's foot of sorts."

"Just don't use it. Hand ride."

"Sure, sure." The jockey glanced at Tierney, as if he doubted the owner's authority to give orders.

When a radiant Francine returned to track side and took Mark's arm, it only irritated Charlie more. He hadn't even noticed *her* presence, Charlie thought. He only had eyes for Francie.

In truth, Mark had spotted her bright curls standing out among the drably dressed men when Madoc had burst from the road into the meadow. Only Francine's strong grip on his arm had kept him from rushing to Charlie's side. The cold, wet ride to the cabin the evening before had successfully extinguished his temper. And in a calmer frame of mind, he realized that he didn't believe a word Charlie had flung at him. Something had happened to cancel out everything he'd

148

done the last two days to smooth over that disastrous first day. Mark was sure her change of feeling wasn't tied to the apparition at the séance. It had been something else, something totally unrelated to the hauntings.

He was still distracted with worry over her. The little hothead refused to let anyone watch out for her, and she refused to listen to any warnings, to admit there was danger involved in ghost hunting. Even he hadn't recognized the full extent of the threat until Mary MacCrimmon's ghostly hand had reached toward Charlie.

He'd just have to backtrack and pick up his trail from yesterday afternoon. She'd trusted him then. She could learn to trust him again. Hopefully, in the interim, he would figure out why Mary had tried to possess Charlie after inhabiting Kat Rinehart's body.

Jaffee took Pride around the track at a trot twice before he told Tierney he wanted to let the colt out. The jockey's arrogance rubbed the trainer the wrong way. When he'd worked with the man at Garrison Ranch, his attitude had been one of respect. Still, Jaffee was one of the best. Reluctant, Tierney gave him permission to gallop the young stallion.

Mark surreptitiously watched Charlie, considering the best way to word an apology. But his attention swung to the track when Francine gave a cry of dismay. Across the small track, he could see Jaffee's arm rise and fall, the riding crop in his hand striking the straining chestnut. He heard Charlie's gasp as the whip fell again.

Pride was stretched out, his hooves spitting mud in his wake. His eyes rolled in terror and he twisted, trying to tear the reins from the jockey's hands. Jaffee fought him until training won out over the colt's fear. As they rounded the turn, the chestnut's speed slackened in response to the reins. They went past the spectators, still flying, then turned and cantered back.

"Fantastic speed," Jaffee called. "I'd like to see how he is with other horses, Tim. I'm definitely interested," Jaffee shouted to the trainer.

Pride halted obediently next to his owner. "Ready to talk turkey, MacCrimmon?" the jockey asked, an eager grin on his sharp face.

Mark's hands grabbed the front of the little man's heavy pullover and lifted him free of the saddle. "Talk is too good for you, you bastard," he grated out, his voice dangerous and low.

Jaffee's fingers dropped the reins he'd been too surprised to loose. He dangled above the ground, helpless. Pride bolted down the track, his eyes still wide and rolling in fear.

"Hey, so I forgot," Jaffee sputtered. "That colt has got untapped speed. I know it."

Mark's face was dark with controlled fury. "I'd like to break every bone in that sneaking little body of yours, Jaffee. Horsewhip you with your own stick."

"Mark!" Francine screamed. Her knees and forearms showed damp and muddy where she'd fallen on the slippery track, running to prevent a disaster. "Put Nick down!"

Mark wasn't focusing on her, or on the terrified man in his hands. Charlie's bright curls caught his attention as she ran after and caught Pride's dragging reins on the opposite side of the field. If Pride reared and fought her . . .

Jaffee fell into the mud.

Charlie snatched the reins, but made no effort to get closer to the chestnut. She cooed softly to him in an effort to calm him. Jimmy arrived a moment later, panting from his dash.

"Easy, Pride," he puffed. "It's all right now."

Almost on the boy's heels, Mark vaulted over the inner rail from the infield. "Is he injured?"

Pride whinnied nervously but allowed Jimmy to take his bridle. "Just scared, sir. He'll be okay. What did that jackass think he was doing?"

Mark had already turned to face Charlie. She stood like a statue, Pride's reins trailing from numb fingers. "What the hell did you think you were doing!" Mark shouted at her. "You could have been killed, you little fool!"

Charlie's face grew white with anger. Concern for the frightened colt had sent her chasing after him ahead of the others. She didn't hear the fear in Mark's voice. She responded to the profanity as he continued to berate her.

Burning with indignation, she turned and silently marched off the track, back toward the manor. It was only when she reached her room that she recalled the reason she'd gone to the stable.

Chapter Nine

JACK PULLED THE heavy drapes open in his room. "Well?" he demanded.

"Well, what?" Charlie's pen tapped thoughtfully on a steno book. "You want a critique on that little gem?"

Jack sighed and plopped down on the leather sofa next to her. "At least it rated *gem*," he said. "What did you think of Mary?"

"Very clever," she allowed. "I wonder why I couldn't see her during the séance?"

"Christ, you mean you still don't believe in ghosts?" the cameraman sputtered. "What do they have to do? Hit you over the head?"

Charlie shook her head. "Nope. The MacCrimmons sure have you brainwashed, though. Didn't you notice your specter displayed a remarkable resemblance to Gwen?"

"They *are* related."

Charlie scoffed. "After three hundred years? Come on, Jack. The family resemblance wouldn't be that close anymore."

"It's still possible."

"So is Gwen in a dark wig and costume."

Jack threw his hands up in the air. "I give up! What are you going to use if this is unacceptable?"

Charlie looked surprised. "Oh, I'm using every bit of film you've taken so far. Just a little editing. This wraps up the assignment. It's Friday. We can report back to the station and to our own apartments. Ginny will be glad to see you."

"You're kidding!"

"About Ginny, or about leaving?" She smiled. "We can edit it Monday and film the narrative Tuesday. It'll be sewn up by Wednesday."

Jack was rebellious. "I can't go now. I'm onto the hottest bit of film history . . ."

"Come on. We've overstayed our welcome. We've got our ghost story, such as it is."

"No, we haven't. Not the whole thing. If we did, you'd be convinced there are such things."

"I don't think so, Jack."

He gave her a suspicious look. "What happened to the woman who was set on disproving the hauntings? You seem in an awful hurry to leave, Chuck. It wouldn't have anything to do with a certain laird, would it?"

Charlie glared, her eyes radiating pure disgust. "I don't possess the knowledge or training to *disprove* your beloved ghosts. I'm just not going to *prove* there are such things. Stan, and NAB, I suppose, just want a nice little Halloween show."

The fact that she hadn't answered his last question was an answer in itself. She was running away. The scraps of information she'd gathered weren't enough to make a decent program, much less one that would get her to network headquarters in Chicago.

"Okay." The cameraman shrugged. "For what it's worth, I think we should stay at least one more night. See if Mary puts in another performance, although I don't think she could top last night's."

"Or Gwen can't," Charlie added.

"Damned if you aren't the most stubborn . . ."

"Ah, come on, Jack," she said, exasperated that he was so gullible. "A few wisps of chiffon, a bit of paint, a stage setting conducive to a ghost story, and the right publicity campaign . . . bingo! An apparition everyone swears is the real thing."

"But . . ."

"Take into consideration the fact that Gwen *and* Don were present at every manifestation. That they are the ones who called us in. And that they are eager for publicity . . . any kind, apparently. Why else bring in a news team? Lovell and Kat are the professionals in the ghost business, and from what I understand, neither of our suspects called them in on the job. Imogene Hale, Gwen's mother, sent Kat. And Wynstand told me Mark is responsible for Lovell's arrival."

Jack was silent, contemplating his fingertips as he slumped in the cushions. "It does make sense, Sherlock, but I'm not convinced. Why does Mary keep after you?"

Charlie twisted in her seat, pulling her cold, stockinged feet up to tuck them beneath a plaid, wool blanket. She noticed a mud stain that she had missed on the cuff of her jeans. Her caked boots had been conscientiously removed at the terrace door before she padded back to her room.

It had been a mistake to go to the track that morning. The sooner she left the manor, the better it would be for all concerned. She just had to make it all sound plausible to Jack now. His love affair with the MacCrimmon ghosts wasn't healthy, anyway. This belief Jack had, that one of the non-existent creatures had its sights set on her, proved it was past time to evacuate the premises. "I don't think she's been after me. Even if she was," she placated, "it's because they've made it look that way in an effort to convince me that she's real. The reason is still publicity."

"Which you intend to give them."

"After a fashion. Maybe not the way they expected."

"The Arden Touch, huh?"

She grinned. "The Arden-Donahue touch, I'd say."

"Flattery won't get you anywhere with this ol' boy, Chuck. We need one more night."

"No, we've got enough."

"You're that convinced it's a hoax and not real?"

"Jack," she said fondly. "What else could it be? A rational person doesn't believe in ghosts."

"Don't try to insult me, Chuck. I prefer to be irrational. Just give me one more night in this mausoleum and I'll have your proof, one way or another."

Her blue eyes narrowed. "How do you propose to do that? We haven't got anything but conjectures and photographs of just what they want us to see."

"Yeah, but we didn't lay any traps before." His warm brown eyes danced with mischief.

"Traps?" Charlie pondered the word. She had a partial idea of how to tie together the elements of her story, yet she longed to return to her original concept . . . proving the ghosts of MacCrimmon were no treat, just a trick. If they remained one more night, she'd have to continue socializing with Mark. Could she stand to be so near him and not let things get out of her control? "I like the idea, but the MacCrimmons are probably anxious to be rid of us."

Jack snorted at such an idea.

"All right," she capitulated. "If Mark agrees, we'll stay."

A wide smile split Jack's face. "No sweat. I'm glad you've crossed him off the list of suspects, Chuck. I really like the guy."

She looked up, startled. "I haven't absolved him of guilt. He's in it just as deep as his brother and cousin."

"Naw," Jack drawled. "He's on our side. If we have a side."

"But . . ."

"You can't make a case against him," the cameraman continued. "It won't stick."

She certainly didn't need a champion for Mark. "He's

obviously hand in glove with them. Just look at his actions last night at the séance."

"He's nuts about you."

"He claims to see and talk to ghosts," she insisted.

Jack leaned forward and flicked the end of her nose with his forefinger. "So do I, and you love me, don't you?" Jack teased.

Charlie laughed. "Sometimes I'd cheerfully strangle you," she said.

The cameraman stretched and got to his feet. "Good. Now that that's settled, let's get down to lunch and proposition our haunted host."

Mark wasn't the only one who was haunted, Charlie thought dismally. She would be haunted by his memory the rest of her life.

Charlie dawdled changing clothes before following her ravenous partner down to the dining room for Mrs. MacLynn's daily luncheon buffet. Due to his early rising, Mark was usually the first family member to arrive at the table and Charlie had hoped to miss him by arriving late. Instead, their arrival was simultaneous.

"There you are!" the little housekeeper cried. Her indignant glare made it uncertain whether she refered to the man with muddy boots and a heavy growth of beard at the terrace door, or the slim reporter in the doorway to the hall. "You should both know better," Mrs. MacLynn berated. "Grown men and women acting like children and missing breakfast!"

"You," Mrs. MacLynn turned on her employer, "sitting in Timothy's office drinking coffee all morning, no doubt. And you," she turned, hands on her wide hips to face Charlie, "hiding away, watching Mr. Donahue's films. I'm surprised either of you bothered to come for lunch!"

Since both of her victims seemed ready to flee, Mrs.

MacLynn issued orders that they sit as she piled plates with food.

Only Don and Jack remained in the room. Empty place settings showed where Gwen and the other guests had eaten. Charlie wished she'd come earlier. Perhaps with everyone present she wouldn't have been as conscious of the disheveled man on her left. She felt tongue-tied. Yet she wanted to tell him so many things, things she hadn't told anyone. Things that, if he knew, might make him understand her attitude, her refusal. If she started, she was afraid she'd babble, falling over herself as words spilled out. And yet she couldn't. All she'd do was make a fool of herself over a man who already had Francine Voight waiting in the wings.

"How'd Jaffee handle Pride?" Don asked, sipping a final cup of coffee.

"Like an S.O.B.," Mark said. He leaned back for the housekeeper to deposit a laden plate before him. "Francie's riding him. We signed the contract this morning."

Charlie stared at the large salad before her, no longer hungry. Francine Voight had lost no time.

"I thought Grady had her all tied up," Don remarked, unaware that every word twisted the knots in Charlie's stomach.

Mark didn't miss the tightening of her lips. "Loopholes," he told his brother. "And there's no conflict of interest. Grady doesn't have any three-year-olds slated for the season. We contracted her just for Pride."

"Trust Francie not to miss an opportunity," Don said.

Charlie read a double meaning into his statement.

"I've got a meeting in town. Do you need anything to go to the television station or to be picked up, Charlie? Jack? It's on my way," Don offered.

It was the perfect opening for Charlie. "No, thanks, Don," she said. "We'll be leaving tod . . ."

Jack didn't allow her to finish. "I want to shoot one more

evening before we wrap it up," he butted in, letting his fork hover over a second piece of pumpkin pie. "If that's all right with you, Mark. Then we can clear out tomorrow."

"Stay as long as you like," their host answered.

Triumphant, Jack grinned at his partner. "Thanks."

Charlie was anxious to get away from MacCrimmon Manor. "We can leave today," she insisted. "We don't want to intrude any longer than necessary."

Jack frowned at her.

"You aren't intruding," Mark said.

He was unconcerned whether she stayed or left, Charlie thought. Why should he care? Francine had already moved into his life.

"Stay until you have what you need," Mark added.

Charlie pushed at a piece of lettuce with her fork, making a pretense of eating. Jack could remain, but she had definitely worn out her welcome. It would be best if she left. But could she tear herself away? It was one thing to make a logical decision. It was another to follow it when her emotions demanded she stay, just a little while longer.

Don got to his feet. "Oh, by the way," he said. "Lovell wants to set up a séance around ten tonight."

Charlie sighed. It began to seem that circumstances wouldn't allow her to follow her head. "I suppose more footage can't hurt."

"I think there's more film in the van," Jack began.

"No."

The word was followed by a startled silence. Charlie wondered if she'd imagined the laird's quiet declination.

Don was nonplused by the quiet word. "You can't mean that, Mark."

"Yes, I do. There will be no more séances in this house," the laird said, his attention on his meal.

"Why?" Don sat down abruptly. "I thought we wanted to find out why there have been so many appearances lately."

Mark met his sibling's eye. "We did."

"Did?"

"Mary told us the reason. Now that she's had her say, I doubt if she'll be back. For a while at least."

"That's easy for you to say," Don insisted. "It's Gwen and me she's been after."

"And Charlie," Jack added.

"Jack . . ." she remonstrated but was overshadowed as Don nodded magnanimously.

"I'll grant you that," he said. "But . . ."

"No buts." The unflinching tone of Mark's voice made it very clear the metamorphosis back to laird was complete. His word was law. "They don't bother me. You and Gwen will be leaving soon, so it'll end. Mary and the pack stay with the house. You'll be free of them."

Don wasn't buying. "You called Lovell in, and now you won't allow him the means to conduct an investigation," he argued.

Mark's patience was worn thin. "Ah, come off it, Don," he ordered. "Lovell doesn't need a séance to search for ghosts. He'll leave beside himself with joy over what he's got."

"A few recordings and measurements?"

Mark's grin was sardonic. "Kat Rinehart. Haven't you noticed? They've become as close as Siamese twins since last night. Inseparable."

Clearly irritated by his older brother, Don abandoned the issue until he had more firepower. He was the stereotype of a politician, Charlie decided. Never actually admitting anything, evading decisions, beating others to death with half-promises. Gwen would always back him up, as she undoubtedly would over the séance question. Once the Channel 5 team was gone, it wouldn't be worth their while to pursue anyway.

Don glanced at his Rolex, checking the time. "Listen, I'll be late if I don't leave now. I'll talk to you about this later."

Mark shrugged and returned to his meal.

With Don gone, only the news team and their host remained at the table. Jack polished off his pie and scraped back his chair. "If you'll excuse me, I have a few things to pick up in town." He winked conspiratorially at Charlie and dashed out the door.

"I suppose those faces were meant to convey something to you?" Mark said. "Since Jack already said he had enough film, and has recently converted his room into a darkroom and viewing studio, my guess is you're finally planning to set a few traps."

The accuracy of his statement added to her depression. She almost expected him to read her thoughts. Almost. Fortunately the ones that troubled her the most remained hidden from him. "I haven't the least idea," she lied, chasing a cherry tomato through the scattered lettuce on her plate. Anything to keep from looking at him.

"I'm surprised you haven't done something along those lines before this," he continued.

"I was distracted," she murmured.

Mark stiffened at the reminder, at the way she threw words back in his face. "I see," he grated out. "Once you've caught your human agency, you'll leave."

"I'll leave now, if you want. Jack can finish without me." She pushed her plate back. It was still covered with salad. If she didn't leave immediately, she'd make a fool of herself by sobbing out her love for him. She already was a fool—a fool to forget past lessons, past pains. A fool to fall in love with Mark MacCrimmon. The laird. He was a man so out of her sphere that she'd been insane to ever dream he could care for her.

He caught her hand as she rose. "Charlie," he said, his voice soft. "Please don't leave."

She had to escape. The touch of his hand and the caressing way he said her name held her captive.

"I'm sorry I yelled at you this morning. Thank you for your concern over Pride," he apologized. He was an ass mouthing inanities when he wanted to crush her in his arms, taste again the sweet nectar of her body opening trustingly to him.

She glanced at him, then away. "It's all right," she whispered.

Mark caught the sparkle of tears in her luminous eyes. Tenderly he took her chin between his forefinger and thumb and turned her tragic face up. He gazed into the swimming sadness written there. "Ah, Charlie, bonny Charlie. Say you forgive me," he coaxed and kissed her tenderly.

He was driving her crazy. Every sense screamed with longing as she fought to remain passive.

With an effort, she turned her head away from the intoxication of his kiss. "There's nothing to forgive," she declared, her expression stony. "If you'll excuse me, I have work to do."

She always seemed to be using her job as a shield, he thought. She could forget it if she wanted. She had already done so that one glorious afternoon. But if she felt out of control of a situation, she exhumed her assignment to hide behind. *The Job* governed her life, leaving him without a place in it. "Certainly," he said, sarcasm covering his impotent frustration. "I have a lot to discuss with Francie myself."

Charlie's chin came up. "Well, I wouldn't keep her waiting if I were you. I understand she can be quite hot . . . tempered."

Mark smiled cheerfully at her, the startling white of his teeth such a contrast to his dark, unshaven jaw. Damn, she was jealous! That catty pause spoke volumes. Perhaps if he fed the fire a bit, it would explode. When the dust cleared, and the inevitable, thoroughly enjoyable making up was over, he'd tell her that he loved her to distraction, that he wanted her by his side the rest of his life. Together they'd fill the manor to the damn rafters with children and make those noxious specters hysterical with joy. But first, he had to get past her barricade. He needed to see her pixie face animated in fury, to see the flash of hatred in the sapphire depths of her eyes as she railed at him like a shrew.

"Francie?" he mused, then sighed. "Yeah, you could say that. A real wanton. Never a dull minute. I'd better get down to the stable." The fact that Francine Voight had left the estate hours ago didn't matter. This was war, and he was confident that he would emerge the victor, no matter how many underhanded ploys were necessary.

A blaze of fury banished the tears and set Charlie seething as the door swung closed behind him. How dare he continually throw that . . . that . . . bitch in her face! The woman was an opportunist, hungry for power and position in the racing world. She was just like Farley, using Mark as a ladder to her goal. Neither of them, Farley or Francine, was good enough for him. Neither loved him the way she did. It was only because she loved him that she sacrificed him, rather than pull him down as she had Phil.

No, that was wrong.

Phil had told her she was poison. She didn't believe it. Or did she?

In a sleep-like daze, Charlie left the dining room and took the stairs to her room. Her failed marriage was all long dead and buried, faced and dealt with, wasn't it? Phil was a jerk and always had been. She knew his accusations weren't true, so why did they raise their ugly head now and disturb, confuse her? It didn't have anything to do with Mark, anyway. It was her. She'd foolishly withdrawn from the world, throwing herself into her work. She'd been successful at it, too. If the offer came from NAB for a Chicago slot . . . no, *when* it came, and she would accept it, she'd stop shutting people out. Then, perhaps, she wouldn't fall in love with the first man to kiss her. She'd let lots of men kiss her, hold her. Maybe in their arms she could forget the fascination and ecstasy she'd found with the laird of MacCrimmon Manor.

Charlie was thankful when the sun finally decided to set. The afternoon had been an eternity. She had repacked her belongings and tried to make notes on the program, but depression overcame all her attempts at work. It wasn't just Mark she was going to miss. She would miss Mrs. M's cheerful greetings and scoldings. She'd miss the beautiful view of rolling pastures and grazing horses. She'd miss the roaring fires, the drafty halls, and the solid, cold stone of MacCrimmon Manor itself.

And all of that was ridiculous.

It was impossible to become so attached to a place in just a few days. It was impossible to fall in love at first sight. But that was exactly what she had done. It was the disreputable cowhand who had awakened her, not the cool host she'd been introduced to later. That they were one in the same, only confused things.

What was real, the only thing that had been real the last five years, was her work as a reporter. She had worked hard for her position as Channel 5's main anchorperson and didn't relish leaving it, even for the network, if she were honest with herself.

She'd go to Chicago though. She'd be a fool to turn down such an opportunity. Roots could be planted anywhere. The manor proved that. It might have looked incongruous once to find the ancient house on bluegrass, but it was still a home filled with people who cared about each other. From employees to employer, they were one family, a clan, even if common bloodlines no longer tied them together. The fealty was there. The love.

A home. It was something she hadn't really had, or known she'd wanted, in a long time.

The dissatisfaction went further than her marriage. Perhaps even back past her parents' divorce, to their unhappiness. As a child she'd felt responsible for their fights. In adolescent innocence, she'd chosen the wrong man and accepted the guilt for his failings as well, thinking they'd been her own.

Charlie stared at her reflection in the glass as dusk colored the fields beyond her window. She had no idea when she'd been drawn to the view or how long she'd stood there without really seeing it. What she did know was her dogged determination had been reborn. She would turn this assignment into one hell of a story. She'd move to Chicago, New York, Timbuktu and begin a new life, one where she no longer hid from her emotions and needs. Work was still important, but she now recognized that it did not fill her life as she had believed it could.

When she heard Jack return across the hall, she marched over, ready to throw herself into his ghost-catching plan.

Dinner was subdued that evening. Four of those gathered resented Mark's refusal to allow another séance. The news team's thoughts were on the trip wires and cameras they would set up once the household settled down for the night. Only Mark and Bill Wynstand were in good spirits. Wynstand kept up a running monologue about the history of the house and family. He'd spent the day amid dusty diaries, letters, and other memorabilia Mark had shown him in the spacious attics of the manor.

Charlie attributed the contented expression in Mark's eyes to an afternoon with Francine Voight. Jealous, she wondered if he had taken the woman jockey out to the cabin, as well.

"It was a total waste of time," Neil Lovell decried after dinner as they gathered once more in the lounge. "Not one decent impression, although we walked the place over three times."

Kat Rinehart looked worn out with the effort to keep up with her latest male interest. "It was all so jumbled," she murmured. "So many impressions crowding in upon each other." Her hands flew to illustrate a bombardment of ideas. "If only one would have been clear, it would have given us something to work with, wouldn't it, Neil?"

"Something." Lovell sighed. "Anything at this point. I don't understand why there are no strong impressions. The clans were a violent people and the house has witnessed numerous incidents that should have left some memory images. The spectral automation witnessed last night was possible only through the emotion or hysteria released by Mary MacCrimmon Douglas three centuries ago. It is extremely curious that only four of us actually were sensitive enough to see it, yet the camera picked up the form in vivid detail."

Charlie sipped at her glass of wine. She noticed that Mark, in his self-appointed role of bartender, never asked her what she wanted to drink. Since the first night, he had simply poured white wine for her. Or forced whiskey down her after séances. "With that in mind, Neil," she said, "what are your findings on the séance? Or is it too soon to hope for a report?"

Lovell shrugged. "They weren't very significant, I'm afraid. If only we could have another sitting, I could gather more readings as a comparison."

As one, they turned to where Mark leaned casually against the highly polished oak bar. "My decision stands. No more dabbling with the spirit world. Mary won't show again and neither will Dad."

"You can't be sure . . ." Lovell began.

"I am." Mark smiled. "The message has been relayed. We won't have anything but anniversary walks now."

Jack sat up so abruptly that he almost spilled the stein of beer in his hand. "Damn," he muttered, then as he realized Charlie's narrowed cat's gaze was upon him, he relaxed again. "It was nothing, don't sweat it."

Mark picked up a bottle of bourbon. "Another round?" he asked. Wynstand jumped at the offer.

Charlie found it hard to keep her eyes averted from the tall, dark-haired man behind the bar. The midnight lights that danced in the depths of his eyes lured her from her purpose. Had she ever known a man who found humor in so many aspects of life? One who could swing from fury to tenderness and back again in a fraction of a second? He wore a Machiavellian grin, as if he realized the battle that raged within her heart and knew the outcome. It wasn't going to be what Mark expected, she was sure.

Jack was the first to stretch and declare it a night. "These long ghost-chasing hours are catching up with me." He yawned. "Night, y'all."

In quick succession, the others found reasons to excuse themselves. Don had papers to read. Gwen had calls to make. Kat and Lovell just escaped with sheepish glances. Rather than find herself alone with Mark once more, Charlie bid Wynstand and her host a good night and followed the couple out.

When she slid into Jack's room a little while later, she found the television turned to Channel 5. The familiar form of Ty Cutter, the weekend anchor, surveyed a stack of papers on the screen as the recorded opening credits ran. ". . . News at Eleven with Charlie Arden. Russ Lopez with sports and Leslie Rogers, weather."

Cutter looked up on cue and smiled ingratiatingly. "Good evening. Charlie Arden is on assignment. In Lebanon today . . ."

Cutter was itching to get her job. He did a fair job, but never exerted himself to dig deeper than the surface on any story. He didn't have the charisma to keep her ratings, either. Still, he was the obvious replacement for her when she went to the network. It grated to have him slide so easily into the chair she'd worked so hard to land.

Jack was stretched out on the sofa, his eyes closed, apparently unaware that the set was even on. When she switched it off, his eyes opened.

"Fantasies do come true." He sighed. "Well, not quite." He eyed the dark sweater and jeans that hugged her slim figure. "It's supposed to be a transparent, black negligee."

"Very funny. What would your wife say if she heard you talking that way?" she scolded.

"That I'm very healthy," Jack assured her.

"Sick is more like it," Charlie said. "Ginny is a gorgeous creature and much too good for you. Besides, I don't own a black negligee."

He leered theatrically and twirled an invisible mustache. "I could make do without it," he said.

"Ha, ha. When do we run the trip wires?"

"Always business. Not until everyone's back in their own room."

Charlie perched on the arm of the sofa and ran a hand through her curls. "At that rate, we'll be here all night. I doubt if either Don or Neil are in their own rooms."

"In that case, now's as good a time as any," he said, getting to his feet. "We'll do this corridor through the gallery and down the main staircase and the hall."

"Won't that take more cameras than we have?"

Jack shook his head. "Correction, Chuck. More that we had. I borrowed the rest this afternoon."

They worked quickly and quietly, stringing fishing lines at ankle height and shoulder height, connecting it to specially adapted cameras, some with flash attachments, some with infrared night lenses. The corridor was completed by the time they heard Wynstand retire to his room off the gallery. Charlie suggested waiting until Mark was in bed as well, but Jack vetoed the idea, remarking. "If you want to tuck him in, Chuck, I can run the rest of the line myself."

Charlie told him crudely what he could do with the suggestion.

"Okay, okay. It was only a thought. Besides, he's in a different wing. I thought you knew that."

She hadn't but wouldn't stoop to asking how *he* knew it.

The last camera was set, the last line attached so that only the flashlight beam in her hand picked up the network of wire, each set ten to fifteen feet apart.

"Now what? We wait?" she asked.

"Personally, I'm going to sleep," Jack said.

The flashlight traced one fine filament after another. "It looks like a giant spider web," Charlie commented. Even though it was lowered, her voice echoed in the great hall.

"This ameba will make it through," Jack assured her. "Anything without a light won't. Coming up?"

Charlie shook her head and switched off her flashlight. "I'm too keyed up. Think I'll take a turn on the terrace first."

Jack shrugged. "Okay. Just be careful coming back up."

"As if I wouldn't," she scoffed.

She waited until he had ducked, swerved, and stepped over every trap before moving to the dining room and out the terrace door. The night air was cold and damp. It made her shiver, though it cleared her head. Hugging herself for warmth, Charlie gazed out over the moonlit landscape. Clouds still scuttled across the broad face of the autumn moon, but somehow she knew the morning would be clear. The sun would shine brightly as she left MacCrimmon Manor.

What was there about the manor, the people, the land, that made her such a different woman from the one who had driven up the lane four days ago? That woman had been self-assured, confident, content in her career-bound world. Now she was just a girl again, confused, full of self-doubt and afraid of the decisions she had made. Once she had run to her father's comforting arms, but she doubted his love could soothe the anguish in her heart anymore.

She should have sensed his presence, recognized the stain of cigarette smoke in the air. It wasn't until Mark spoke that Charlie realized she was no longer alone.

"Are you really leaving tomorrow?"

She didn't turn around but steadfastly stared at the moon-drenched paddock and stable. "Yes."

"Why?"

"I have to."

"Do you want to?"

Charlie clamped down the impulse to shout the answer her heart made with every beat. No, she never wanted to leave. She just knew she had to, had to put distance between Mark and herself, to sort out the changes he had made in her life. But she couldn't tell him, couldn't admit her weakness. "It's very beautiful," Charlie said instead.

"That's not what I asked," Mark insisted.

"You know there is no easy answer," she whispered more to the night than to the man standing in the shadows so near.

He sighed. She could almost feel the expelled breath stir her curls, he was so close. "Perhaps I'm not asking the right question," he said.

Charlie turned to face him. "I think we have enough for our story. It's time we left."

The orange glow as he drew on his cigarette was too faint to illuminate his shadowed face. He exhaled, the smoke wafting toward her in the breeze. "That's not what I'm talking about," he said.

"I have a deadline."

The cigarette sailed over the terrace wall, a small shooting star in the night. There was that damned job again! "And I love you," he said tightly, his anger barely controlled. "I thought I said it in my actions. What do you want me to do? Shout it from the rooftops?"

"I love you," she whispered and wondered why she'd told him.

She was glad when he didn't make a move to touch her. Mark's voice was low, ringing with emotion as he answered. "Don't leave, Charlie. Stay."

She managed a light laugh. "As easy as that."

"Yes, as easy as that." His voice caressed her, tempted her.

"What about Francine?"

"She's a damn good rider."

"Nothing else?"

The flash of his wolfish smile in the moonlight somehow reassured her. "A calculating bitch. I prefer fiery vixens." His arms went around her gently then, and Charlie didn't resist. She rested her cheek against the soft wool of his sweater. "I still can't stay," she said.

"Because of Francie?"

Charlie's sunset curls tossed in denial. "No, because you're who you are and I'm . . . I'm me."

"Because we fight?" Mark pursued

"No, although we do."

His coal-black eyes sparked provocatively. "Not always, sweetheart. We also make love beautifully together."

"Mark, don't," Charlie breathed, her voice ragged as he traced the perfect features of her jaw and touched her lips with his rough, calloused fingertips. "Don't make it harder than it is for me."

"I've loved you from the moment I saw you perched on the fence purring at Pride," Mark said. "You have a very seductive voice, my darlin' Charlie. I almost took you off to the cabin then."

His lips followed the course his fingers had traveled, driving away the little resistance she strove to maintain. "But you didn't."

"I wanted a willing partner," he answered. "And when I

got her, she was glorious. I haven't been able to get her off my mind."

Charlie found herself returning the soft kisses that Mark rained on her lips, her cheek, her brow, her eyes. "You'll forget once I'm gone," she insisted.

"Absence makes the heart grow fonder."

"Not always," she whispered. He would forget, but she wouldn't. Not ever.

"Then let's not try it," he urged. "Stay."

"I can't." The hoarse longing in her voice turned the two words into a plea for things to be different.

Mark's arms crushed her willing body closer, warming it with awakening passion. His mouth covered hers, hungry, demanding, devouring her faint opposition. "Damned if you aren't a stubborn witch," he rasped. "Have it your way then. Leave. But tonight is mine, Charlie. Tonight you are mine."

It hurt more, she found, to have his accept her decision. The hard, muscular feel of his body against hers, the taste of tobacco in his kiss, the ardor and pain in his eyes were all memories that she would take with her tomorrow. She wanted more. One more token. Arms entwined around his neck, she met his lips. "Yes," she murmured. "Tonight I belong to you and you to me."

His lips silenced any further talk. Mark swept her up into his arms and carried Charlie back into the warmth of the manor.

Chapter Ten

CHARLIE SLID FROM Mark's arms. Her feet sank into deep pile carpet, the only modern, and thus incongruous, feature of his room.

A few personal items were flung about, but otherwise she felt the room had looked much the same for the last five centuries. It was obviously the chamber of the laird, not a specific man but a continuous succession of men. The massive curtained bed, the trunk-like chests, and the ornately carved chairs weren't a reflection of the real Mark MacCrimmon. Yet they were. The heirlooms represented the responsibility he never shirked, the traditions he upheld as head of the family.

She stared at the bed. Generations of MacCrimmon men had slept there, had made love there. Had conceived sons to carry on the traditions, to carry on the line.

He could just as easily have carried her to her room, or his office. But instead, Mark had chosen to bring her here, to his room.

Charlie looked up at him, her eyes brimming with love. Was there a message in his action? Did it matter if there was? Only a few days ago he had been just a name on the sports page to her, the man behind the tartan racing colors. But now . . .

Mark stood on the threshold, waiting for her to make the next move. He was afraid that Charlie would understand why they were in the master suite. Afraid she would not.

Her eyes were solemn as she faced him. Then she crossed to the bed, going as if by design to the opposite side, and began disrobing.

Mark let out the breath he had been holding. Her actions weren't an answer, but then he hadn't asked the question. He knew she had accepted the ghost-hunting assignment to win a promotion to the network. Winning was something he understood. Winning was something he couldn't take away from her. And, by saying a few simple words, words that would bind her to him and to MacCrimmon, he would be stripping away everything for which she had worked.

He followed her, going to his own side of the massive bed and stripping quickly. His eyes never left her. They caressed her as each of her garments dropped to the floor. When he tossed back the sheets, Charlie slid into bed and opened her arms to him.

They came together without words, without preliminary caresses.

"Charlie . . ." he whispered hoarsely.

But she didn't want him to talk, not even to call her name. Too much hung unsaid between them. She was afraid words would be said, and later regretted.

"Hush," she said and pulled his head down to hers. Her lips were open and questing. Her tongue slid over his teeth and deep into his mouth. Her hands clutched at his shoulders, her nails cut into his flesh as Mark deftly took her deeper into a universe of shared pleasure.

As Mark slept, Charlie slid from beneath his arm and out of the massive curtained bed. She had said good-bye to him using her lips, her hands, and her heart. In the morning she would be gone.

For now, she had responsibilities that could not be ignored. It was time she returned to her vigil with the cameras and trip wires. As Charlie dressed silently, she watched Mark's even, quiet breathing. She resisted the impulse to brush a stand of raven hair from his forehead. She had made her decision, and, hard as it was, she knew she would abide by it. The choice was made from a series of logical reasons, just as she had made every move in her career thus far. Emotions didn't enter into it. She had been hurt before. She had to keep reminding herself of that. It wasn't reasonable to consider that her feelings for Mark, or his for her, were anything more than an infatuation. It wasn't logical to believe she could fall deeply in love in a few days' time. But she wanted to believe it. Wanted to with all her heart.

With one last, fond look at her sleeping lover, Charlie turned and left the room.

It was the closing of the door that woke him. Still drowsily sated from love-making, Mark reached for Charlie.

The sheets were already cool where she had lain.

He sighed and closed his eyes. She hadn't understood, after all. And he'd found it hard to say the words that would make her stay. Once, he had said *marry me* to a passionate woman, and she had destroyed his dreams. He knew in his heart that Charlie Arden was different. Yet the words stuck in his throat.

Fool, he berated himself. Go after her. Tell her you love her again. Tell her you want her to share your life, your name. Tell her you want to have children with her. Tell her that without her you are only half a man.

Mark sat up against the pillows and reached for a cigarette. The only way he could possibly say all those things to her was if Charlie herself wanted to hear them. And until she was no longer bound to MacCrimmon Manor by the need to turn in a ghost story to North American Broadcasting, he knew Charlie wouldn't allow him a chance to tell her anything.

He needed to discover a pattern to the hauntings, to find the link that he'd missed so far in trying to second-guess the reason behind the increase in paranormal activity.

Was the presence of three family members of a similar age in the household the main issue anymore? Considering the attempts Mary MacCrimmon Douglas's shade had made on Charlie, it no longer was a valid excuse. Besides, Gwen's connection to the MacCrimmons was diluted by two generations of MacDonald and Hale blood. He'd been grasping for explanations to ever entertain the notion.

The evening Mary had reached out to Charlie had been one hell of a way to end what had begun as a wonderful day, the day he first made love to her.

What was it that drew Mary to Charlie? Her appearances had been repeated and increasingly strong. Jack's pictures of Mary outside Charlie's room had been taken the night he had invited her out to the track to watch Pride. He had left her feeling encouraged. Walking away from Charlie that night had been one of the hardest things he'd ever done.

And Mary had retraced his steps to her door.

Mark drew thoughtfully on the cigarette.

It hadn't been Mary's first visit though. He was sure that she had been the faint reflection Jack had recorded that first night in the hall, the evening he had kissed Charlie in his office. Christ, he'd thought she was going to capitulate to him that night. She'd clung to him, answering the urgency he'd felt, then had torn herself away, running up the stairs to her room as if he'd been Lucifer himself.

Mark's lips twisted wryly in self-derision. He'd stood in the office doorway a long time that night, listening to the remembered echo of her footsteps in the hall.

The hall . . .

Damn!

Mark sat up straighter. That was the clue he'd missed. Curse him for a blind fool!

He crushed out the butt of his cigarette angrily in the ashtray at his bedside then reached for his jeans.

Mary had appeared at each of the locations of his run-ins with Charlie in the manor. He'd kissed her in the hall, he'd kissed her in her room. And, damn it, the day he made love to her, Mary had tried to touch her, had actually gathered enough energy to materialize during the séance!

The connecting factor was him! The stronger his emotions had been over Charlie, the stronger Mary had grown. He'd been giving her more power every time he touched Charlie.

And Charlie had just left his bed.

If there were a manifestation tonight, it would be the strongest to date merely because they had made love in the manor, had expended God only knew how much psychic energy for Mary to use.

He didn't bother with shirt or shoes. Mark dashed out of the room then paused undecided in the corridor. Where would Jack have set his traps? The entrance hall? The corridor in the guest wing? Where?

The gallery was ice cold. A draft disturbed the long, heavy damask drapes that covered the narrow window casements. No moonlight penetrated the dark. The only illumination was that of Charlie's flashlight as she picked her way past the maze of fishing line.

It was eerie. One of the twin automatic cameras hummed as it shot infrared pictures at two-minute intervals. Charlie doubted the sound was loud enough to alert anyone, but it sounded loud to her and grated on her nerves.

She shivered and eased herself into a dark corner. The purr of cameras had always been something she could concentrate on. She used to focus on the sound to calm and soothe her nerves before going on the air. Tonight, it had a negative effect.

She sat on the floor, hugging her knees. How nice it would have been to stay pressed intimately against Mark's hard body, their legs entwined beneath the sheets. If only things were different.

The humming sound was louder. No, it was a murmur, she realized, and it came from further down the corridor, from one of the guest rooms.

Charlie's eyes had adjusted to the dark, but she kept her flashlight in hand, ready to use it to illuminate her culprit, or swing as a weapon, as the case may be. Silent, she maneuvered around the trip wires.

The sound came from Kat Rinehart's room: voices, hushed and secretive.

The wood was too thick to allow her to hear exact words when she pressed her ear to the door. But a slow turn of the well-oiled latch eased the door open.

Kat was well into her trance. Lovell and Gwen were plying her control, Linette, with questions. Don sat on the edge of his chair, his whole body straining forward, eager to learn Linette's answers.

The control returned only cryptic replies, repeatedly stating, "He comes." Who *he* was she would not clarify.

Charlie eased the door closed. No further information for her story could be gathered from joining the conspirators. Since her suspects were occupied, she saw no reason not to make herself comfortable. By leaving her own door open, and pulling an armchair over . . .

This time it wasn't a sound that distracted her. A pale glimmer of light shimmered in the corridor. It was moving toward her. Jack's flashlight? No, he'd said he intended to sleep the night away, his cameras working for him.

The light paced slowly forward. It came abreast of her and continued past, unaware of her dark, clothed form as she pressed flat against the wall. It was a foot in diameter, Charlie calculated, and without substance or form. And it was growing. As she watched, it lengthened, broadened, began to stretch wispy tentacles from a forming torso.

Unbelieving, frozen to the spot, Charlie saw the light become a human form. A man.

And he was passing through all the trip wires!

Hansel and Gretel, the cameras, were clicking in tandem, alternating minutes now, but in the sixty seconds between their shots, details of the ghost . . . or whatever it was . . . would be lost!

Galvanized into action, Charlie ran down the corridor, tripping the cameras herself. In her haste, she passed through the man's right side. Incredible cold froze her left arm, leaving her shaken. A wave of emotion rushed at her, catching her unaware. The despair and shame were painful in their intensity.

Charlie forced herself to stumble just ahead of the apparition, the cameras whirling into action, flashing, humming, as she sprung each successive trap along his route.

She could distinguish features now. Sad, tortured, colorless, unseeing eyes looked out of a haggard yet young face framed by long, carefully curled hair. An elaborate fall of lace spilled from the front of his coat and covered his hands except where he clutched the pommel of the long, unwieldy claymore he carried. The apparition distained the tartan or kilt. He wore satin knee britches, patterned stockings, and highly polished buckle shoes.

His step lagged as they crossed the gallery and neared the wide main staircase. Charlie found she was crying, gulping for breath raggedly, as her tears flowed. Despair gripped her, was more than she could bear. Yet the apparition's countenance was resolute. Only Charlie's footsteps echoed in the tomb-like silence.

As they reached the stairs, the form quickened his step

and brushed past her, again causing Charlie to experience the cold of death. Shuddering, she grasped the banister as he marched down the stairs. The trip wires remained in place, not even quivering as he passed.

"Oh, dear God, I can't," she whispered. "I can't. Don't."

The elaborately dressed gentleman seemed to hear her. He paused, turned back, and smiled over his shoulder. It wasn't at her but at something behind her. Charlie spun but found only the inky, empty gaping mouth of the corridor at her back. Quickly she turned back to the apparition. He had continued his even pace down to the entrance hall.

A new wave of despair hit Charlie. One she recognized had nothing to do with contact with the spirit. Her story, the most unbelievable part of it, was walking away, unfilmed, and she was helpless, held in place only by an agonizingly tight grip on the banister, frozen to the spot by her fear of the shadow figure that descended the stairs.

Below, another form stepped from the shadows. A very substantial one with a large camera resting on his shoulder, his eye pressed to his lens.

Jack!

Charlie breathed a sigh of relief then straightened as the ghostly figure vanished before her eyes.

"Damn it!" Jack exploded. "Where'd he go? It's his anniversary walk!"

Charlie wilted, sitting down on the top stair. "I forgot about that," she said. "And they told us he'd be walking tonight, too!"

"But he didn't finish it!" Jack insisted. "Why the hell . . ." His voice trailed off, then he started forward. "Look out, Chuck! Behind you!"

Charlie turned. In the corridor a new figure had appeared.

The woman wore her long hair down, cascading over the shoulders of her pale, floor-length gown. She smiled warmly at Charlie and glided forward, her arms outstretched.

Charlie backed away until her back was pressed against the wall. Fear welled in her breast and she screamed in terror.

"MAAARRRKKK!"

Mary MacCrimmon Douglas shook her head slightly, as if admonishing a child. She moved closer.

And suddenly Charlie realized that she no longer feared the apparition. She experienced a warm feeling, one of affection, a kinship with the long-dead spirit.

She and Mary wanted the same thing! Instinctively Charlie knew Mary had never been a threat to her, as Mark and Jack had believed. Mary only wanted Charlie to know she approved. The caress she'd given the reporter's cheek at the séance, the one Charlie had not felt but had seen recorded by the camera, had been an affectionate gesture.

Charlie stared at the pale, floating form. "My God," she breathed. "You are real!"

Mark's heart was in his throat as he rounded the corner from the adjacent wing in answer to Charlie's cry. Mary was advancing on Charlie. This time, Charlie hadn't dropped into a trance state. She was staring at the ghostly form, her eyes wide, her back pressed to the cold stone wall.

He jumped forward, placing himself between the woman he loved and the specter.

"RUN!" he shouted at Charlie.

Instead she grabbed his arm, pulling him with her away from the now fading shade. As quickly as she had come, Mary MacCrimmon Douglas was gone.

Mark sat on the edge of his chair, staring at the wide-screen television. The ashtray at his side was filled to overflowing. His hand shook as he lit yet another cigarette, his eyes glued to the set.

He had told himself that he wouldn't watch the show. It

had been a week now since Charlie had run from the manor. A week in which he picked up the phone a dozen times a day and replaced it without ever making the call.

When Mrs. MacLynn had mentioned the day and time that North American Broadcasting was airing the program—one they had obviously approved to rush it into a prime-time spot in such a short time—he had promised himself that he would not give into the temptation to watch it. What did he care how it had gone? The mere fact that it was on the network proved that Charlie had received her well-deserved promotion. It also meant that he had lost her. Her career had meant more to Charlie Arden than he had.

On the television screen an outdoor view of MacCrimmon Manor appeared. The camera, it seemed, had been mounted behind the wheel of a car, Charlie's bright Impulse. The gleaming, apple-red hood was the only bright spot in the picture.

"Allhallow's Eve, Halloween," Charlie's disembodied voice said. It was authoritative, sultry, and haunting. It put a knot of longing in his stomach.

"The one night a year that thoughts turn to ghosts, goblins . . . things that go bump in the night. And haunted houses. Mansions, to be exact. This one, transported from the shrouded depths of the Scottish Highlands to an estate outside Louisville, Kentucky, nearly seventy years ago, came completely furnished . . . and haunted."

The camera traveled the murky interior, exposing every nook of the hall, touching on each gruesome implement of war, each aging portrait.

Damn. He'd donate the whole collection to Wynstand tomorrow.

On the screen the picture dimmed. Darkened. There was the eerie echo of footsteps. "But there are no such things as ghosts," Charlie's voice said.

Mark stubbed out his cigarette and reached for the bottle

of bourbon on the table. He should turn it off, stop torturing himself. But he didn't. The whiskey burned all the way down his throat.

A match flared in the black screen and became the grotesquely lit face of Mrs. MacLynn. ". . . or are there? We shall see," Charlie purred.

The clip came from the original, unsuccessful séance, but it had been cleverly edited to the second sitting. Charlie's narration dropped off, allowing the real-life participants to develop her plot. Once again Mark watched Linette's controlling spirit be replaced by the fiery Mary MacCrimmon Douglas.

"The séance was carefully controlled and run under scientific specifications by Dr. Neil Lovell, a Duke University parapsychologist, and Katrine Rinehart, a professional psychic medium" Charlie's voice continued.

They had edited the asinine message from his father out of the events, Mark noticed with relief. And Angus had gotten his wish, after all. Francine would be riding Pride. But comparing Charlie to a mare . . . Mark was glad no one else had realized what Angus's comment about "the filly" being a breeder had meant.

"Were the messages, the personality of Mary, really from beyond the grave?" Charlie demanded. "There were doubts. After all, there are no such things as ghosts." Her voice continued to carry a haunting note of its own that undermined the frequently repeated phrase. As the last word died away, the incredible figure of Mary MacCrimmon Douglas began materializing. As she filled out and reached toward Charlie, the screen went to a commercial.

Mark lit another cigarette. Watching it all happen again was sheer hell. Yet he stayed where he was.

The story resumed moments later. The ghostly, transparent, and slightly luminescent hand came within an inch of Charlie's nose before Mark watched himself leap to his feet, his chair falling over backward in his haste, to bodily drag Charlie from the table. The film picked up the fear on his face and in his eyes as he stared at the camera.

He'd been looking at Jack, he reminded himself, but took another swallow of whiskey all the same.

The disembodied form of Mary MacCrimmon vanished. Charlie's voice led the story into flashes from the many interviews she'd conducted. It was easier on his emotions to listen to the droning voices. Lovell explained the measurements he'd recorded. Wynstand gave a bit of historical background, and various MacCrimmon employees told of their own experiences with the ghostly inhabitants of the manor. Although the three MacCrimmon cousins had given on-camera reactions, their comments had been blatantly cut from the show.

She hadn't given the name of the estate either, Mark realized. He smiled. She never had planned to do so. She'd been so convinced that it was all a play for publicity on their part.

Trust Charlie to do the unexpected.

From the interviews, still photographs of the first two visitations flashed by. Twice Charlie's recorded voice declared there were no such things as ghosts. She even went on to tell how the mysterious light in the hall could have been duplicated and the ease with which a form such as Mary Mac-Crimmon Douglas could be created.

Charlie'd been a busy girl since she'd left him.

After the final commercial break, Charlie's voice returned although the television screen showed only a dimly lit corridor. "On the night of October nineteenth at two A.M. we were sure we had caught the human agency creating the ghostly forms. Cameras with trip wires were set to catch the artificial specters. I waited, watching, on the upper floor while my cameraman kept vigil below in the main entrance hall."

Hansel and Gretel, the team of untiring cameras, had caught the first glowing beginnings of the male apparition.

In a series of quickly flashed still photos, the story built to a fever pitch. Mark watched as fear, pain, despair, and agony registered on Charlie's face in each photograph. Her narrative had receded. The moving pictures Jack had taken showed the specter begin his decent, then vanish.

In all the times he'd watched Claymore's reenactment as a boy, Mark couldn't remember an anniversary walk that hadn't been completed. Lord Claymore, the specter, should have continued down to the hall and committed suicide, falling on his sword. The event itself was grisly enough to watch. The fact that it hadn't occured this time was even more frightening. Claymore had failed because Mary has usurped his place.

Mark had heard what had taken place before his arrival from Jack Donahue. But seeing the rapid materialization of Mary behind Charlie on the stairs still startled him. He heard again Charlie scream his name and watched in horror as Mary advanced on a cringing Charlie. Then Mary smiled. And Charlie had returned the smile!

Through clever editing, Jack had cut Mark's own arrival on the scene but retained the gentle figure of Mary as she disappeared. The screen held the final picture, showing a partially materialized form. Then Charlie walked before the blow-up, frozen frame.

"Are there such things as ghosts?" she asked the audience. "Can we communicate with the dead? It's impossible to answer either of these questions based on the events at the manor. No history was found to document the strange phenomena. No scientific facts could explain it. What was it that night? We leave it to you to decide. Personally? I don't know what it was. After all, there are no such things as ghosts. Or are there? This is Charlie Arden." Slowly, her form before the picture of Mary MacCrimmon faded away, leaving only the backdrop. Her voice was an eerie echo.

Mark finished his drink as the credits rolled. Charlie

deserved the promotion to network headquarters. But it meant he'd lost any chance of a life with her. His business was based in Louisville. Hers would now be in Chicago.

The remote control wasn't where he usually left it so he decided to stay before the set a little while longer. To watch her one last time on the eleven o'clock newscast.

". . . News at Eleven with Charlie Arden," the announcer said. Mark didn't hear anything more. He stared at the animated face of the woman he loved and had lost.

Local events, sports, weather. They all went by without Mark being cognizant of their content. But when the weather girl leaned on the news desk and mentioned that she didn't know how Charlie could be so calm after her experiences in the haunted house, Mark began to pay attention.

Charlie smiled. Not at the weather girl, but at the camera. "It wasn't that bad," she said. "In fact, if I were asked, I'd return to the manor tomorrow."

The sports reporter shook his head and gathered the papers before him.

"That's it for tonight," Charlie declared. "Join us tomorrow at five and again at eleven. Until then, this is Charlie Arden."

As the credits began to roll, Mark picked up the phone.

The MacCrimmon estate was even lovelier than she had remembered, Charlie thought as she drove her car down the lane. The meadows were variegated shades of green and brown. Wildflowers still waved at roadside. The tall, leafless trees were welcoming sentinels that stretched their arms over the road sheltering her. In fact, the air itself was more invigorating. Or did it just seem so when you were in love?

It had been so long since she'd first fallen in love. And the amazing thing was, she doubted it had been this wonderful with Phil.

At the top of the final incline, she stopped to stare down at the brooding manor. How had she ever thought it ugly or unwelcoming? It was beautiful, stately, solid. Home.

Unable to wait a moment longer, she put the car back into gear and drove up to the main door.

"It's good to have you back, lass," a beaming Mrs. MacLynn greeted her. "I've put you in the same room. Why don't you go down to the stable? I'll see to your cases."

Charlie didn't need a second invitation. She let herself out the terrace door and tried to keep from running down the slope to the paddock.

"Ah, I see you're ready, Miss Arden." Tierney nodded, looking over her low-heeled boots, jeans, and sweater. "Brietta's ready and waiting. You just follow that trail across the fields."

It was like being on a scavenger hunt.

Quickly she swung into the saddle while the trainer held the roan's bridle. "It's a fine day for a gallop, isn't it, Miss Arden?" He smiled.

Her dimple appeared in response. "It's a glorious day," she declared.

Brietta was fresh and eager to run. Charlie bent low over the mare's neck and let her mount take the bit.

Brietta seemed to know the way. Her hooves ate up the turf, drumming the packed dirt, perfectly in tune to the excited beat of her rider's singing heart.

The station switchboard had taken the message. It merely requested that she return to MacCrimmon Manor due to new developments.

A woodland flashed by on her right, a field of dry stalks disappeared to her left, and still the mare ran. Their headlong rush slowed when the high, white fence came into view.

Charlie heard the sharp whistle over the wind. Brietta answered it, slowing to a trot, bringing Charlie alongside the gray horse that waited patiently next to the tall man in faded jeans, work shirt, and low-crowned Stetson.

Charlie fell into Mark's arms and lost herself in a blaze of wildfire as he kissed her hungrily.

Behind them, Pride snorted, irritated at being ignored. Then he wheeled and trotted off to the other end of the paddock.

"Back where we started," Charlie sighed, watching the beautiful young stallion.

Mark grinned. "I'm a sucker for nostalgia."

Her eyes drank in his beloved features. It had only been a week since she'd seen him, but it felt like a lifetime. "Why did you think Mary's ghost was a danger to me?" she asked. "She never was, you know."

"But I didn't know," he insisted. "You were being so . . ."

"Stubborn?"

Mark laughed. "That's a kind word for it. I knew that Mary wanted you to stay and I was afraid she would possess you so that her will would override yours."

Charlie caressed his lean cheek. "Mary knew what I wanted long before I did," she said. "She gave me one hell of a story, though."

He hated to ask, but he needed to know the outcome of the broadcast. Was Charlie's return to MacCrimmon just another interlude, or was it the beginning of a brighter future?

"Didn't you get the promotion?" he asked carefully.

Charlie smiled tenderly. He sounded so unsure of himself. Mark, the man who controlled a private empire. "I turned it down."

Mark's spirits rose. He wasn't going to rush his fences, though. "Any special reason?"

"Just one," Charlie said. Her lashes dipped coyly. She glanced at his lips briefly before meeting his eyes. "Finished with the questions?"

The love shining in Charlie's eyes gave him the courage to take the step he had avoided for so long. Mark's arms tightened around her, molding her to his hard, muscular frame. "Just one," he echoed, hoping her answer would please all the residents of the manor, past and present.